DEGREES OF ACCEPTANCE

INTERNATIONAL BESTSELLING AUTHOR

VIA MARI

TABLE OF CONTENTS

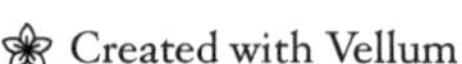 Created with Vellum

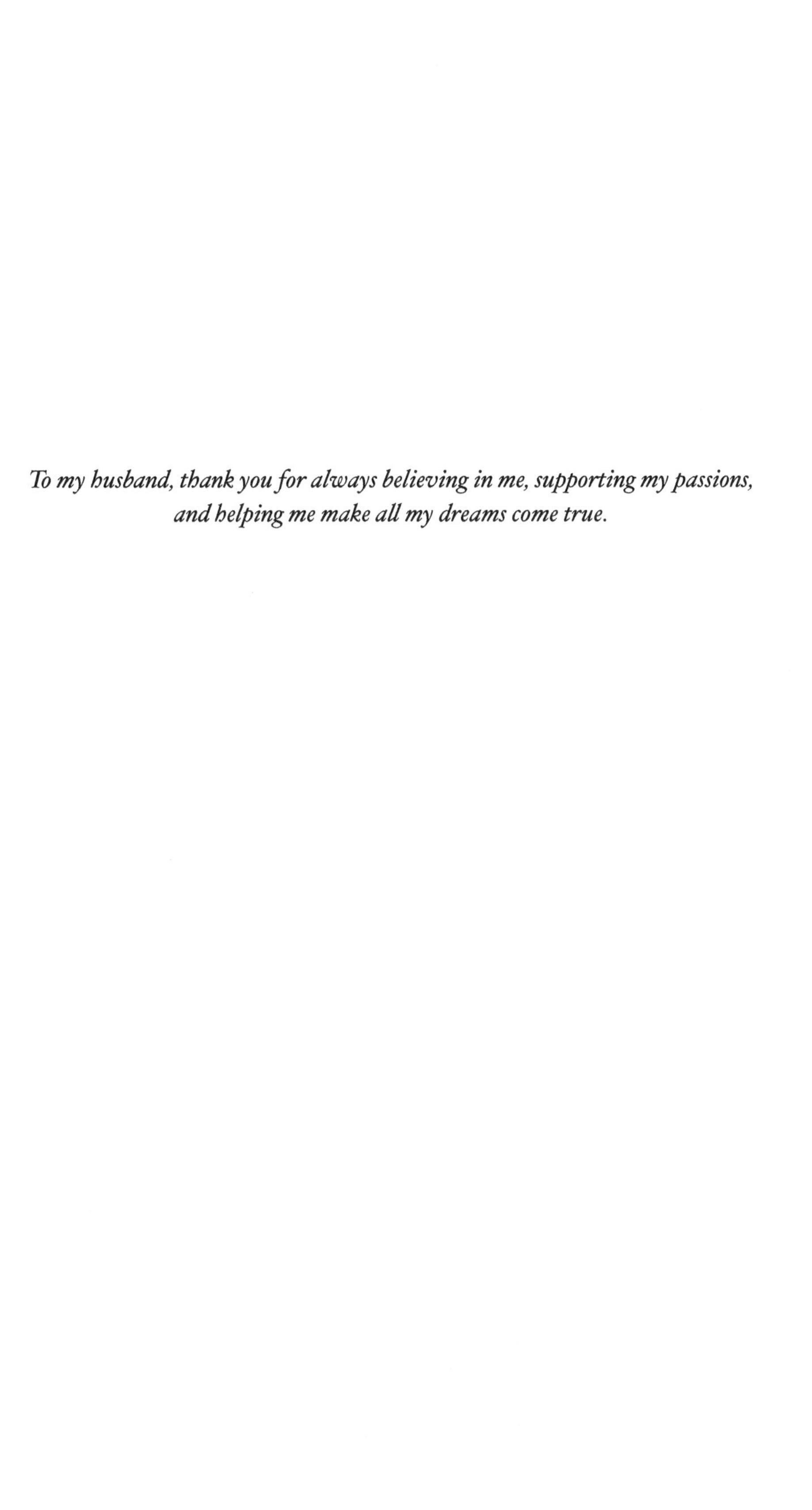

To my husband, thank you for always believing in me, supporting my passions, and helping me make all my dreams come true.

ONE

His intense dark green eyes are dark passionate pools as he holds me close and our breathing returns to normal. He sweeps me into his arms and carries me still nude from the living room desk into the bedroom, carefully placing me on the bed before lying down beside me.

"Baby, what made you decide to stay?" he says, leaning up on one elbow. I admire the features of the man that in such a short time has come to mean the world to me. His sandy brown hair is disheveled from our lovemaking. The broad angular jawline is set, and his intense green eyes are waiting for a reply.

"I can't imagine my life without you, but at some point, you're going to need to tell me the truth. We shouldn't have any secrets between us," I say, wincing as I try to curl into his arms.

"Easy, Baby," he says, repositioning me so my head can rest against his shoulder. My pain medication is starting to take effect, and I am becoming drowsy. "Rest your eyes, Katarina, and let me tell you a story," he says, pulling the comforter around us.

"Last year Prestian Corporation was getting close to reaching an agreement to build a new factory in Saudi Arabia. Prince Alfreita invited me aboard his ship to finalize the deal. When our business was concluded his helicopter took me from the Persian Gulf to Saudi, and I flew home from there. Shortly after I left, we learned the ship was commandeered, and Interpol found one of the largest shipments of cocaine ever documented being transported in its hull. Interpol questioned everyone, but Alfreita pointed them in my direction, and I was a viable suspect given my financial status. I didn't have anything to do with it, Katarina. I was never charged because there was no evidence of my connection, but I'm still a prime suspect, and they have been watching our teams extremely carefully. Alfreita's people still believe we tipped Interpol," he explains, wiping the tears of relief from my eyes and kissing me gently on the lips before I fall asleep in his arms.

It's been almost three weeks since the accident. The long-sleeved teal colored dress I've chosen offsets my long auburn hair and bright blue eyes. I pair it with a multicolored scarf and brown boots, mentally preparing for a fight with Chase over my decision to go back to work.

His eyebrows rise as I walk into the room, and his eyes brazenly scan my body, lingering while taking in my apparel. My skin heats under his steady gaze. "You look beautiful, today. Where are you going, Katarina?" he asks from the table where he's working on his Mac.

I take a deep breath, renewing my resolve. "I'm starting to feel much better. I haven't even taken ibuprofen the last couple of days. I need to get back to work," I say, bracing myself for what is sure to be an argument.

"Why not sign on from here so you can nap later in the day?" he asks.

"Chase, it's been almost three weeks since the shooting. I want to go back to work." How can I explain to him that with all the craziness in the last couple weeks I just need to feel normal again?

"I'll let Jay know we're heading in then," he says, pulling out his cell phone and taking me completely by surprise. I expected a full-blown argument as protective as he has been since the shooting. This is so anti-Chase. I wonder if he's absorbed in something and I've just caught him at an opportune time. I can feel some of the anxiety in my body start to wane and take a seat next to him for breakfast.

I'm excited to be returning to work, especially since I'll now have an office at Prestian Towers instead of at Torzial. It will save hours of drive time each week. I wonder what his employees will think of me. The tabloids were relentless for the first couple weeks after my shoulder surgery with story after story about our relationship and I'm sure his employees have read at least some of the articles. I especially hated the one which referred to me as a gold digger set out to ensnare Chase for his money. Maybe that is why I'm feeling so anxious this morning.

"Jay will have teams in place shortly," he says, disconnecting his call and pulling me back from my thoughts. He pours us each a cup of coffee. "Are you going to eat something?" he asks, taking in the still empty plate in front of me.

Maybe that will settle my nerves a little. I select a bagel and strawberries. "What, no homemade french toast or pancakes?" I ask, teasing between bites, and still trying to gauge his mood.

"Hmm, unfortunately, my skills in the kitchen are slightly limited," he says, grinning. He checks his phone and frowns. I assume it's a text from Jay. "More paparazzi," he explains, seeing the question on my face.

There are only a few reporters downstairs, nothing like the barrage we have encountered in the last few weeks. Jay, head of Chase's security team and Matt, who is assigned specifically to guard me, guide us from the door to the backseat of the Jaguar with minimal fuss. We reach Prestian Corp, a chrome and black glass sky-rise towering over those around it. Chase maintains hold of my hand as we enter the executive suites on the top floor, briefly stopping to chat with several people along the way.

As we reach the end of the corridor, he opens a set of double french doors. "This is your office, Baby," he says. His dark green eyes are wide and watchful. The room is spacious with a contemporary high-gloss black desk, sleek in design with a matching credenza. A large window behind the desk provides an almost panoramic view of the surrounding high-rises and river below.

"Chase, it's absolutely breathtaking," I say, stunned by the incredible expanse of river winding between the buildings below.

He pulls me into his arms and kisses me on the lips. "I'm glad you like it. Let me show you the adjoining areas," he says, guiding me into the conference room which has the same view as the office. The remaining walls are covered in whiteboards and equipped with overhead projectors. I count sixteen chairs and iPads around the long oval conference room table.

"Chase, it's amazing, but it's so much more than I need," I say, taking in all of the technology.

"Baby, I had it designed especially for you. This way you have everything you need to collaborate and bring large groups together without ever having to leave the building," he says as we walk back into my office.

"Chase, did you make this entire space for me so security would not be an issue?" I ask, pretending annoyance and failing miserably as I see the look of amusement in his eyes.

He scoops me up and places me on the conference room table. "Shhh, that's enough," he says, laughing. "I want you to have space near mine conducive for your work. Although, I do have a few ulterior motives, which is why I had a bathroom and shower installed," he admits with a mischievous grin. "Now get some work done so we can go home at a decent hour. You'll probably tire in the afternoon," he says, kissing me briefly before leaving me to get acclimated to my new workplace.

I have a large monitor on my desk and a sixty-inch screen hanging on the wall across from it. I shake my head as I slide into my chair and investigate the Mac system in front of me. I am logged onto the network in relatively no time and become submerged in the medical facility work.

I wonder if Terry, the architect assigned to the Prestian Corp Medical Center project has any of the documentation he needs from the user group event. I doubt his boss, who was fired by Chase shared the information with Terry.

I shiver as I recall Mark's retaliation and rub my shoulder where surgery was required after his attempt to kill me was thwarted by Chase's security team. I try to keep my mind off of the ordeal with Mark and set about organizing all of the materials.

TO: TPartes@Martel&Sons.org
　　From: KMeilers@TorzialConsulting.org
　　CC: CHPrestian@PrestianCorp.org,
　　JWarling@TorzialConsulting.org

HI TERRY,

I am happy to hear you'll be working on the Prestian Medical Center. I have attached the workflows and all the other documents from our work group.

We are in the process of procuring additional land, and those specs are included. As you review the information, please feel free to reach out to me with any questions. Looking forward to working with you on the project.

Thanks,

Kate

Kate Meilers, Project Consultant
Torzial Consulting Firm

TO: KMeilers@TorzialConsulting.org
　　From: CHPrestian@PrestianCorp.org

YOU'VE BEEN WORKING all day. I thought surely you would need a nap this afternoon. Are you ready to go home?

C. **H. Prestian**
　　Chief Executive Officer, Owner
　　Prestian Corporation

TO: CHPrestian@PrestianCorp.org

From: <u>KMeilers@TorzialConsulting.org</u>

I DON'T KNOW where the time went... I can be ready and finish up later.

Kate

Kate Meilers, Project Consultant
Torzial Consulting Firm

TO: <u>KMeilers@TorzialConsulting.org</u>

From: <u>CHPrestian@PrestianCorp.org</u>

You've had a full first day, Baby. You still need to rest. I'll pick you up shortly.

C. **H. Prestian**
Chief Executive Officer, Owner
Prestian Corporation

I LOOK up to find him standing in the doorway observing me. He is impressive, tall at about six feet two, with a frame that is muscular and lean, his custom-made suit hangs on his body impeccably. I reluctantly drag my eyes from his body.

"The office suits you very well, Katarina," he says. His mouth is set in an amused quirk, and I wonder what he's thinking.

"I absolutely love that you designed it for me, Chase."

"I'm glad it pleases you," he says, his eyes capturing and holding mine. The magnetism between us is palpable.

He pulls his cell out of his pocket, appearing annoyed at the silent intrusion and answers it briskly. I pack up my belongings and grab my purse preparing to leave as he talks. After a few moments, I can sense his growing agitation.

"No, we are not changing our position. If they want the company and employment, they go by the same rules as everyone else. We've worked through similar challenges in other countries. Sid, I'm not compromising the workers hours and benefits. Hold steady, and let's ride it out. They are not about to risk losing a high-tech company that will put thousands to work. The government knows it's the only chance they have to provide an infrastructure for future innovations. Hold firm," he says, before disconnecting.

"Where were we now... " he asks, pulling me close and capturing my lips lightly with his own. "Katarina, I love the way you feel in my arms." I glance around to see if anyone is nearby and immediately feel him stiffen. "Let's go home, Baby," he says, guiding me toward the elevators. Jay apparently knows where we are headed without any direction from Chase.

The short drive to the condo is unusually quiet, and I contemplate his mood. We are soon in the elevators of the most impressive sky-rise in Chicago on our way up to the penthouse condo that he calls the city apartment. I smile at his reference as we walk through the five bedroom luxury condo overlooking the skyline and Lake Michigan.

"How's your shoulder, Baby?" he asks as I drop my purse and belongings on the bar stool chair.

"It feels a little tight, but otherwise, much better," I say, feeling fortunate the gunshot did not damage anything but minor blood vessels.

"Would you like a glass of wine?" he asks, regarding me warily.

"Yes, please," I say, curling into one of the large overstuffed couches. He's clearly got something on his mind. "Why are you so quiet, Chase?" I ask as he pours each of us a glass of wine.

"I'm thinking about your issues with being involved with someone you work with. You seemed to like the office and proximity of it to mine, but I felt your hesitancy both this morning and afternoon with public displays of emotion. It's apparent while you trust me physically, you don't have that same confidence where your emotions are concerned," he says, watching me intently.

"Chase, what do you mean by that exactly?" I ask, annoyed that he could tell and not sure how I want to approach this.

"You were clearly uncomfortable with me kissing you at work. Even when there was no one around, you weren't comfortable."

It's the first day that I haven't napped since undergoing surgery; I'm tired and ill-prepared for this depth of conversation. I immediately feel put on the defensive. "Chase, we have known each other for less than a few minutes of our life. In that time I have had to deal with you lying to me about who you are, then learn that you are not only someone I work for but that you are the owner of the company that employs me."

He starts to interrupt, and I hold up my hand. "You are a multibillionaire and with that comes a ton of baggage. Just the security alone is overwhelming, but let's not forget the fact that you were suspected of drug trafficking. You seriously don't think I trust you after I learned all of that, and still moved in with you? Do you think I would let someone I don't trust tie me up and do the things you do to me?" I demand, furious and unable to hold the tears back any longer.

He pushes the hair from my face and gently wipes a tear that has escaped. "You are obviously still upset I was not honest with you upfront, and I deserve that. But, it does not, in any way, negate or diminish what I said. If you trusted me, we wouldn't be having this conversation right now."

"I do trust you," I say, leaning in to kiss him, wanting and needing to connect with him.

"Katarina, our physical and emotional relationship should stem from a deep level of trust with each other, and right now we need to work on developing that," he states flatly.

I flinch, feeling his cold rejection of my offer. "Katarina, your mother's experience left you with scars, and you've never had a partner that you could trust. Unfortunately, I started the relationship on false pretenses. I've explained my reasoning, but no less, it's added to your fears.

Katarina, I'm not interested in having half a relationship. I want your unbridled trust. That's the only relationship I'm interested in having, so we are going to have to work through your fears. Otherwise, your lack of trust will end up driving us apart, developing into jealousy, fear and any number of other manifestations," he states.

I'm so out of my league. "What am I supposed to say, Chase? I wasn't prepared to answer questions about us kissing in the hall. Don't you think the employees need time to get to know me? All they know is what they've read in the gossip magazines." Surely he must see how I feel.

"Baby, if you trusted me you wouldn't worry about something like that. You're scared of my public display of affection because you can't imagine how I will react if employees gossip. I would never let them or anything hurt you," he says solemnly.

It's now or never.... "I don't doubt you, Chase... and I do trust you. I'm just not sure how to tell you what I'm dealing with right now. When I was in the hospital, my mom shared a lot of information that I'm still trying to absorb."

His eyes raise and turn to concern as he sits beside me and takes my hand. "You can tell me anything, Katarina," he says.

I need to confide in him. I'm just not sure what he will think about having a relationship with the daughter of a mafia hit man. My mouth feels dry as I begin to speak. "My entire life I thought my mom had an affair at work, and the break-up is what caused us to move around, for me to lose my friends and the reason she cried herself to sleep at night. When she came to the hospital, she told me that wasn't the case. In fact, the guy I thought she was having an affair with actually helped her get a new job because she didn't feel safe and needed to move again." I know I am beginning to ramble, and my heart is beating fast.

"Katarina, slow down, Baby... breath," he coaxes, pushing the hair out of my eyes and pulling me into his lap. "Tell me," he urges.

"I never really knew that much about my father. My mom left him before she even knew she was pregnant, so he is out there somewhere and doesn't even know I exist." His hand is soothing...rubbing my back.

"I know I told you that there's nothing to dredge up in my past, but it appears that may not be the case," I say.

"Baby, we'll find him. It's a small world," he says, trying to console me.

"No, you don't understand, Chase. He can't know I exist, or my mom could be in danger."

"Why would that put your mom at risk?" he asks, lifting my chin to meet his eyes. "Trust me," he says.

"Chase, my mom told me everything when I was in the hospital. She left him and ran away because she learned he was the eldest son of an East Coast crime syndicate. My mother told me that he put a hit out on two people, and she overheard the conversation. That's why she ran, and if members of the syndicate find her, they will kill her," I say, looking into his eyes, trying to gauge his reaction. *Will he still want to be in a relationship with me?*

His eyes are hooded and controlled giving nothing away. "Katarina, I'm going to want to talk to your mom. We can go for a visit or have her come to Chicago, but I'm going to need the details."

"I don't know how she'll feel about that," I say warily. How can I explain to him that she only told me because I confided in her that I thought Chase may be a criminal? She left my dad because she found out about his criminal activities, but never stopped loving him and didn't want me to make the same mistake with Chase, so she broke her own vow of silence and told me.

"Your mom probably needs to talk to you as much as you need to speak to her. Call her, Baby," he urges.

TWO

I awake the next morning, early, unable to sleep. He gave me the perfect opportunity yesterday, and yet I couldn't tell him how I feel about him. He's sleeping peacefully, and I manage to slip out of bed, find running clothes and brush my teeth without waking him. It's barely four a.m., and I briefly contemplate going for a run without security but quickly abandon it at the thought of Chase's reaction.

I text a message to Jay's phone and am surprised by the immediate response.

Message: Is it too early for security to go with me for a run?

Reply: Nope... five minutes. Can you take the lakefront route?

Message Sounds good. Thanks, Jay.

Reply: You bet.

It takes a few moments for my breathing to sync, but I'm soon running at a good pace, with only the music and my thoughts. I contemplate the night's discussions and replay them in my head. Is he right, do I not trust him? Is that why I can't yet tell him how I feel? What if he doesn't feel the same? Maybe that's why I feel insecure. Do women just fall in love faster than men?

The park path along the lakeshore is dark and quiet this morning. A scattering of seagulls is scavenging for food along the edges of the blue-grey waters which appear relatively calm. My cool down song comes on, and I walk the remainder of the way, enjoying the briskness of the fall day against my skin. The doorman greets us with a friendly "good morning," as we enter the high-rise. Chase is in the kitchen cooking when I enter the condo and seems quite at ease with himself. "Are you hungry?" he asks, grinning widely at my look of surprise.

"I am ravenous, and it smells delicious," I say, dragging my eyes from him to the meal he is preparing. Chase in the kitchen with lounge pants, no shirt and no socks on is hot.

"I'm making omelets with peppers, onions, mushrooms and ham. It's one of the few things I know how to cook. I thought you might be hungry, you've been running for over an hour," he says.

"Did I wake you? I was trying to be quiet," I say.

"You didn't wake me. Jay let me know you guys were on the move early," he replies, sliding the omelets onto a serving dish.

"I thought you would be mad at me if security didn't come with me. Otherwise, I wouldn't have woken him that early."

"I would have been furious if you went without them and you wouldn't have been able to sit down for days," he says.

"Hmm, is that all it takes?" I tease, my eyebrows raised in mock inquiry.

"I'm sure some sort of punishment for your disruption of securities' sleep is in order," he says, mouth upturned with amusement as he puts a plate with an omelet, piece of toast, and muskmelon in front of me. He pours us each a cup of coffee as I try my first bite.

"This is superb, Chase. You can cook for me anytime," I tease in between bites.

"My dad will be at Prestian today, and I want you to meet him. He just flew in from New York and would like to take us to dinner. Do you mind staying in the city tonight?"

"No, of course not. Does your dad work at Prestian, too?" I ask.

"He has a suite of offices in the tower, but he and Brian spend most of their time in the New York offices. Dad met Emily last year, and I think they've grown quite fond of each other. She lost her husband about ten years ago, and her children and grandchildren live there, too," he says.

"So you don't get to see him much?"

"We often talk and travel between Chicago and New York frequently. I'll take you with me on one of the next trips so you can meet Emily. She wasn't able to make it this time," he explains.

It reminds me that I really do need to call my own mom. I'm still trying to absorb the fact that I have a father who doesn't know I exist. The hospital visit is the last time I've talked to her since I haven't really known what to say. I've been answering texts, but I just haven't gotten up the nerve to have a full-blown conversation with her about it, yet. "I should call my mom and see if she wants to visit Chicago unless you'd like to make a trip to Naples?" I ask.

"Why don't you and your mom talk about it and whatever you decide is fine, but let's do it soon. I'd like to learn more about your dad and make sure security is appropriately appraised. If she wants to fly up, we'll send one of the jets down to pick her up."

"Chase, I'm not sure if I want to know who he is," I say hesitantly.

"Katarina, you may not want to get to know him or have a relationship with him, but if he and his family were to find your mom, it would lead them to you. The only way I can ensure your safety is to be well informed and have security in place," he says.

My head is spinning with everything that has transpired in the past few weeks. To think I thought Chase was a criminal, and as it turns out, my own father is one of the heads of an organized crime syndicate.

He reaches for his phone. "Chase here... Let them know you've discussed it with me and I'm proposing we discontinue negotiations and are exploring different areas for expansion. In the meantime, put some feelers out and get back to me," he says, disconnecting.

"What's the matter?" I ask.

"Just ordinary negotiations when host countries are required to change their existing labor laws and practices. We are at a critical point, though, ready to buy and rebuild the information and technological services in Basra. It's in an ideal location. It's situated on the southern border of Iraq, on the Shatt al-Arab river and adjacent to neighboring Iran, so it would be advantageous to our government and the people in both communities. You really want to hear about this?" he asks.

"Of course... I'm very interested in learning about your work."

"The country has been war torn, and the infrastructure for information and technology is in great need of upgrading. The negotiations were going well, but we've run into trouble with their agreement to our labor and human resource areas of the contract. It can get a little bumpy at this stage."

"Will you fire all the people and bring in your own?" I ask.

"No Baby, just the opposite. This is a government contract, and the goal is to help them develop an infrastructure and provide more of their own people with skills and jobs," he says.

"I don't understand why they aren't happy then."

"They have certain labor laws or gender specific treatment practices, and we are asking them to give them up to get the contract. They are opposed to the human resource and labor part of the negotiations. They want the ability to treat workers as they choose, and it's something I will never agree to," he states.

"So what is all this talk about not working long hours? It's not even six in the morning, and you're negotiating out of the country contracts."

"You young lady are sassy as ever! Why don't you get showered up? I have a couple more calls to make before I get ready," he states, trying to control his smile.

I kiss him gently and instantly feel the spark that exists between us. "Thanks for breakfast, it was delicious," I murmur.

He captures my lips with his own and then deepens our kiss, pushing my hair back from my face as he does. "Baby, you should go and shower before I do unmentionable things to you," he says, kissing my forehead. "Go," he says, as I reluctantly head towards the master suite.

I dress quickly, apply a little makeup and go in search of Chase. He's at his desk, his hair is still wet from his shower, and he is wearing jeans and a t-shirt. He looks up from the conversation he is having on his cell and pushes a button, mute I surmise, as he begins talking to me. "That dress really looks incredible on you."

"Thank you. Who's on the phone?"

"Just a conference call... Sid's doing all the talking," he says, smiling.

"Jay should be ready to take us in shortly. Dad was going straight to the office, and I need to meet with him about some contracts this afternoon."

In short order Jay has us safely at Prestian, navigating the traffic with skill and experience. "So, I take it I can kiss you goodbye when I drop you off at your office?" he asks, referring to our long discussion last night.

I smile teasingly, "I am going to leave that up to you, Chase."

"A quick study," he says, his eyes holding mine with his gaze. He guides me towards my office and stops at the reception desk introducing me to Mary. "Mary has been with our company for over twenty years. She was Dad's executive assistant until he moved to New York, and still manages parts of his contracting and oversees all of the administrative support. Aside from that, she is also a very close personal friend," he adds.

"Mary, Kate is the project consultant for Torzial and will be working on the new center downtown. If you have not read the papers lately, she's also very special to me personally."

"Kate, it's wonderful to finally meet you. I was out of the office the last couple weeks visiting family, but was hoping to get to know you," she says warmly.

"Thank you, Mary. I'm very pleased to meet you."

"Mary, Katarina has moved into the newly remodeled area. Would you be able to assign someone for administrative support? I'd like it to be full-time. See if there is internal interest and backfill if you need to," he says.

"I'll post the position, and if you like you can help with the interviewing process," she says to me.

"Chase trusts your instincts and whoever you assign to assist me will be perfectly acceptable, Mary. I don't want to be a burden to anyone," I add, embarrassed that Chase has asked for clerical support to begin with.

"I'll work to get the position filled and in the meantime, if you need anything, please let me know," she says, seemingly pleased with my answer.

He guides me to my office and shows me the space adjacent to mine. "We had it designed so your assistant would be close," he says. The office has a huge window and lovely view of the city, too.

"You think of everything," I say, almost half under my breath.

"That's the way I like it, Baby. Now, I'm going to take you in my arms and kiss you. If my staff sees us, they may talk about it a little bit. In fact, it would surprise me if they didn't, since it's never happened here before. Okay with the plan?" he asks.

"So does a girl have to wait all day for this promised kiss," I tease.

"Oh, you need only ask once, Baby," he says, capturing my lips. His hand is caressing my neck holding me steady, rubbing the sensitive area behind my ear. My skin heats from his touch, and I lean into his fingers. He kisses me gently one more time before releasing me.

"I should let you get some work done now. I need to meet with Dad; he just got in a little while ago. Let Mary know if you require any assistance and try to let someone else do things that you don't need to do yourself. It will provide someone with an excellent job at a good company, and you'll have more time to spend with me."

"And if I don't, I know, you will be renegotiating my contract," I say, laughing.

"You are a quick study," he says, pushing a piece of hair out of my eyes and kissing me gently on the mouth. "I love having you here at Prestian. Text me if you need anything."

I look around the office, and still can't quite believe how lovely it is. I unpack a couple pictures: one of my mom and another one of my best friend, Jenny. The windows are spacious and have plenty of space to hold plants. I plan to go shopping to personalize the space further. I turn on the Mac and open up Pandora to one of my favorite stations and settle in to begin work on the medical center project. The morning flies by and it is already late afternoon before I attempt to catch up on email.

TO: KMeilers@TorzialConsulting.org
   From: TPartes@Martel&Sons.org
   CC: CHPrestian@PrestianCorp.org,

JWarling@TorzialConsulting.org

KATE,

THANK you for the workflows and diagrams. I have asked that we have three architects dedicated to the design of the Prestian Medical Center since there will be two different facilities.

We are in the process of projecting a footprint for each design based on the size of the land. I can assure you there will be more than enough space to put in the Medical Center and any number of other amenities such as parks, water retainments, or anything else the team referenced based on the amount of land Prestian has purchased.

Thanks,

Terry,

Terry Partes
Lead Architect
Martel and Sons

TO: JWarling@TorzialConsulting.org
From: KMeilers@TorzialConsulting.org
CC: CHPrestian@PrestianCorp.org

HI JENNY,

Are you available in the next week or so to get together for drinks or dinner with Chase and me?

Kate

KATE MEILERS
Project Consultant
Torzial Consulting Firm

TO: <u>KMeilers@TorzialConsulting.org</u>
   From: <u>CHPrestian@PrestianCorp.org</u>

I like the plan. The last time I spoke to Jenny we were both worried sick about you at the hospital, and we didn't get properly acquainted.
   C. H. Prestian
   Chief Executive Officer, Owner
   Prestian Corporation

TO: <u>CHPrestian@PrestianCorp.org</u>
   From: <u>KMeilers@TorzialConsulting.org</u>

I THOUGHT you were visiting with your dad. Are you always online?
   Kate

KATE MEILERS
   Project Consultant
   Torzial Consulting Firm

TO: <u>KMeilers@TorzialConsulting.org</u>
   From: <u>CHPrestian@PrestianCorp.org</u>

IT'S CALLED MULTI-TASKING. Hurry up and finish working!!

C. **H. Prestian**
   Chief Executive Officer, Owner

Prestian Corporation

TO: CHPrestian@PrestianCorp.org
  From: KMeilers@TorzialConsulting.org

ARE you always going to be this bossy?? I have a few more emails to respond to and a little more work to do on the time studies.
   Kate Meilers
   Project Consultant
   Torzial Consulting Firm

TO: KMeilers@TorzialConsulting.org
  From: CHPrestian@PrestianCorp.org

YES!! I would threaten you with a good paddling, but that only seems to encourage you.
   C. H. Prestian
   Chief Executive Officer, Owner
   Prestian Corporation

TO: CHPrestian@PrestianCorp.org
  From: KMeilers@TorzialConsulting.org

IF I RECALL, you still owe me one...

KATE MEILERS

Project Consultant
Torzial Consulting Firm

TO: <u>KMeilers@TorzialConsulting.org</u>
   From: <u>CHPrestian@PrestianCorp.org</u>

IN TIME, Baby.

C. **H. Prestian**
   Chief Executive Officer, Owner
   Prestian Corporation

TO: <u>CHPrestian@PrestianCorp.org</u>
   From: KMeilers@TorzialConsulting.org

PROMISES, promises... I seem to recall getting turned down flat!

KATE MEILERS
   Project Consultant
   Torzial Consulting Firm

TO: <u>KMeilers@TorzialConsulting.org</u>
   From: <u>CHPrestian@PrestianCorp.org</u>

. . .

STOP PROVOKING me or I will take you home, paddle your ass and then bring you back to meet my dad.

C. H. Prestian
Chief Executive Officer, Owner
Prestian Corporation

TO: <u>CHPrestian@PrestianCorp.org</u>
  From: <u>KMeilers@TorzialConsulting.org</u>

KILLJOY! I'll try to behave... But I am seriously wet, here.
  Kate

KATE MEILERS
  Project Consultant
  Torzial Consulting Firm

I FEEL him watching me and look up. I can't help notice how his muscles flex beneath his suit jacket and how his pants hang over his lean hips and powerful thighs. "Did you have a good visit with your dad?" I ask, trying to focus.

"I had a great visit, but I was distracted by the thought of your wet panties," he says, walking into the office and locking the door. I feel myself moisten, and my breathing begins to change.

"You know I tried to anticipate everything this space may be used for and designed it accordingly. I installed blinds since I anticipated the need to fuck you in this room, especially when you email me that you are soaking wet," he says, pushing a button that I had not noticed. The blinds fall into place, effectively blocking out all visibility to the room. I am sure he can hear me breathing... God, he is hot. "You designed the blinds with this in mind?"

"Yes, I couldn't imagine keeping my hands off of you at work, Baby," he states, rounding the desk, moving the Mac out of the way. He lifts me onto my desk, positioning my legs so that my feet are resting on his thighs. "You have the most incredible legs. They go right up to that delectable little ass," he says as his hands move up my dress and around my hips, pulling me closer to the edge of the desk. His fingers hook into my panties. "You have a choice to make. You can lift your ass off the desk and let me pull these lovely little panties down, or I can rip them off for you, in which case you will be going to dinner without them," he says huskily.

"Chase, I am soaked. These panties are too wet to wear anywhere, Honey," I exclaim.

He pulls the thin material away from my body and pushes my legs farther apart, watching me as he makes his way between my legs. I can barely breathe, and he hasn't even touched me, yet. It's the anticipation he creates and builds, and finally, his tongue finds its mark.

"Honey," I moan, grasping his hair as he pleasures and teases me. I am lost and with just a few more strokes he brings me crashing down around his tongue.

"Oh, Baby, you were so in need. What made you so hot?" he asks, looking up at me.

I am embarrassed that he asks such intimate questions from that position. "I was in the mood last night, and you turned me down flat," I respond, looking into his eyes.

He sits back in his office chair and slides his zipper down, freeing himself. He grasps me by the waist and eases me into his lap so that I am straddling his body. "Baby, I'm sorry you felt turned down emotionally, but I'll admit you were supposed to feel deprived." He is watching me intently as he positions himself and pulls me onto him, sliding me over his engorged and needy length. "Baby, I want you to ride my cock until I feel you shake at the end of it," he instructs.

I am so turned on. Going slow is hard.

"Easy Baby, all the way down," he urges. His eyes are molten and smoldering.

"Oh, that's so deep," I say huskily.

"Now, again... up and down," he instructs. His hands cradle my hips, helping me gain momentum, up and down, over and over. He kisses the sensitive skin of my neck, nuzzling it as he shifts deeper inside of me. I can feel my body building as he fills me time and time again. "Baby, cum for me," he moans, pulling me down forcibly over his hard cock. I wrap my arms around his neck as I explode again, trembling over the top of him. I feel the power of his release deep inside of me and rest against his chest, trying to catch my breath as he strokes my back and neck. I look up to him, and he is watching me, his eyes like green magnets pulling mine to him. "What are you thinking?" I ask breathlessly.

"You called me Honey twice," he says, almost thoughtfully.

"You don't like it?" I ask pensively.

"No, I quite like it," he says, smiling widely.

"I hope it makes you feel like I do when you call me, Baby," I whisper.

"If we keep talking with you half naked on me, we are not going to make dinner, I can promise you that," he threatens, still stroking my back.

"Seriously, do we have time to run home quick? I'd like to rinse off and put on fresh panties," I say, trying to hide my embarrassment.

"We have time to run home if you don't want to use your shower," he says.

"I don't have any spare panties, and I am not going to meet your dad like this," I say.

"You'll have to keep an extra pair in your drawer," he says, grinning. "Are you done working for the night?" he asks.

"Yes, I am going to create a simulation for the presentation of the exam room data, but I won't be able to extract what I need until morning."

"I'd like to see what you're proposing to share with them. A simulation sounds interesting," he states.

"You take me home so I can wash up and put some panties on, and I will show you the simulation software and what I'm proposing."

"You are a tough negotiator," he says laughing.

Chase is still smiling as we enter the condo. "Baby, you can negotiate whatever you want as long as you let me do that to you. I'll pour some wine while you're getting ready."

I find a hair tie and put my hair up so it doesn't get wet, plug in the curling iron and hop into the shower. I quickly redress and spritz on some perfume, rummaging through the dresser for a pair of panties and find what I'm looking for. A lacy white thong... I can't help wonder how he will like them. I begin putting large hanging curls into my hair, patiently heating each part with the curling iron, add a little powder, blush, lip gloss and apply a light coat of mascara giving myself one last critical look in the mirror before finding Chase.

He sets his drink down as I walk into the room, crossing the distance in seconds. He traces his fingers over the swell of my breasts where my hair rests. "You look absolutely stunning, Katarina" he murmurs appreciatively. "I love the way your hair is hanging over your breasts. I am going to enjoy it, even more, seeing it hang over your bare skin later tonight. In fact, I'm going to have a very hard time thinking of anything else this evening," he says, huskily.

"I wanted to look nice to meet your dad."

"Baby, you always look beautiful. I'll have Jay bring the car around while we finish our wine before I decide to keep you home and all to myself."

Jay navigates the heavy evening traffic. "Chase, what did you tell your dad about us?"

"I told him I met someone in Aruba that I care about, and that you've been living with me for the last few weeks. Is there something else you'd like me to share with pops?" he asks, grinning. I blush, knowing full well what he means.

The restaurant is small, with an old world feel. Chase gives the hostess his name and we are escorted to a dining area in the back of the restaurant. A gentleman with a strong resemblance to Chase stands as we approach. His smile is broad and genuine as he shakes my hand. "You must be Katarina. I've been anxious to meet the young lady that charmed the pants off of my son. You know I don't mean that literally," he teases.

"I'm very pleased to meet you Mr. Prestian," I say, trying unsuccessfully to control my blush.

"Please, away with the formalities. Call me Don," he says with a smile.

His dad has already ordered a bottle of wine, and the waiter is quick to check in with Chase on our needs, pouring us both a glass of wine and waiting to see if it meets with his approval.

"Katarina, Chase tells me you are in charge of the design for the Prestian Medical Center project. You know that center is something I've wanted to see created for years, and I'm excited we're actually going to do it. Chase tells me you pulled together a team of healthcare workers to develop it around the patient experience," he says.

"Yes, they did an excellent job. It's one of the most worthwhile projects I've been part of. When you look back at the things you've done in life, it always feels good to know that you've made a difference in some small way. We held patient focus group sessions before we went into the event and some of their stories were heart wrenching."

"I love your enthusiasm, and I can't think of a better way to design space than to build it around the needs of the patients. A toast. My sincerest best wishes to both of you on this project," he says, and we all raise our glass. I glance at Chase, who has an amused look on his face. I look down and can't help but smile.

Message: Dad approves.

I look up, and he is smiling at me.

Message: And you're blushing.

The waiter arrives to take our order. I order the arugula salad and dusted peppercorn sea scallops, which comes with parmesan risotto, wild mushrooms, and basil oil. I almost laugh as Chase and his dad order the house salad and ravioli, almost in unison. He catches me smiling and gives me an amused look.

Chase tells his dad that I love any type of seafood. "When you come to New York there's a place that has excellent seafood. At least, that's what Emily says."

"That sounds fabulous. I grew up in Florida, so fresh fish and seafood were always plentiful."

The meal is excellent, and the scallops are perfectly seasoned with garlic and peppercorn, and they almost melt in my mouth. The men enjoy their pasta which smells richly of cheese, garlic, and roasted tomatoes. After we're finished, the waiter brings both Chase and his dad a piece of chocolate cake with a flavored espresso icing. I can't imagine how they can eat anymore, or where they put it. Chase slices through the thick piece of cake and places a little of the icing on his spoon urging me to try a bite. I do and instantly know why they ordered it.

"It's sinfully delicious," I murmur, catching his father's amused look. The waiter brings us more wine while his dad regales us with stories about his earlier business adventures. As he talks, I have a chance to take in his features. Chase gets his strong masculine jaw line and frame from his dad, but his eyes are not his fathers. He must have inherited the gorgeous, deep green eyes from his mother. I haven't seen a picture of her, yet, and wonder what she looks like.

I turn my attention back to Chase and almost laugh out loud. He asks for the check, but his dad is clearly not having any of that. Don tells the waiter, "Son, you bring that check back to me. And you put your damn money away," he says to his son, affectionately. Chase raises his hands in mock surrender. "You win, Dad, I'll catch it next time," he says, grinning, clearly enjoying the game.

Chase checks his phone and answers it, clearly annoyed. "Chase here," he says, listening for a few moments. "Set up the meeting, Sid. I'll get back to you tonight with details."

"I take it they didn't pull out," Don says.

"No, and Sid's team has had trouble with the locals," Chase says.

"Son, I think this is one group that may not succumb to your human rights and labor negotiations," he says earnestly.

"Well, they either do, or they will be minus an operation that would bring thousands of jobs to their region" he states coldly. "I am not negotiating the rights of the workers. They will be treated the same way as employees in our other operations. But, I'm going to need to send in another team for Sid," he says, clearly agitated.

As we leave the restaurant, I notice Jay standing at the back of a large stretch limo. Don grabs Chase in a hug to say goodbye and then turns to me. "Katarina, it's been a pleasure to meet you. You are every bit as charming as Chase told me you were," he says, taking my hand

and kissing it in an old worldly fashion. "I've always wanted to do that, but it's never seemed quite fitting before," he says smiling.

"Chase, you take care of this young lady," he instructs before heading toward his own limo and giving us a brief wave.

Chase takes my hand and leads me over to where Jay waits for us, opening the door in the back for me. "You seem to have made quite an impression on my father," he comments.

"Chase, your dad is great. I was really anxious about meeting him. I had pictured him as some conventional board member type," I admit.

He laughs. "My dad stuffy? He's got to be the most laid back multi-billionaire I know," he says with a broad grin. "I'm glad you liked him. I think the feeling was entirely mutual," he states quietly.

He pulls me close to him and kisses the top of my head. "I'm still looking forward to seeing your hair fall over your naked breasts," he whispers in my ear while his hand caresses my ear lobe. I can feel my breathing change and feel myself moistening. I am secretly excited that I've chosen the lacy white thongs and hope he likes them. Jay lets us out to park the car, and I see Peters and Lenny, members of our security detail, in the distance. It's unusual to see them with Jay's team, and I wonder if security has increased for some reason.

As we approach the elevator, two men in suits get in. Chase restrains me with a touch of his hand on my shoulder, allowing Peters and Lenny to get into the elevator ahead of us. We ride it upstairs in relative silence. The men get off on floor twenty-two, and we continue to the top floor.

"Would you like a glass of wine?" he asks, entering the condo.

"That would be lovely, but do you want to tell me what just happened? Who were the men in the elevator? It was apparent that we weren't getting into the elevator without Peters and Lenny."

"The negotiations related to HR and labor is not going as planned for the information and technology center. Sidney and his team have been accosted by locals trying to make a point, and I'm not taking any chances. We are sending in another team, and I have increased security at home for family members which mean there are some additional security measures. One of which is that we do not get into the elevators with strangers without security. I'll go through the list with you tomorrow."

"Now, I was asking if you wanted a glass of wine, in hopes of seducing you to let me see your hair fall over your luscious breasts."

"Oh, flattery will get you everywhere tonight, Honey," I respond, heading into the bathroom to slip into a short lacy white nightgown. I adjust my hair, letting it fall over my breasts and return to the living room. He's settled on the large leather couch and slowly places his drink on the side table as I walk toward him. His eyes take in my body with apparent appreciation, and I delight in the deepening of his green eyes as they capture mine from across the room. "Walk slowly," he instructs huskily.

He stands up before I reach him, and gently pushes strands of hair out of my face, following them down to my breasts. His fingers stroke my nipples through the lacy material until they are erect. He kisses me gently as his hands continue caressing my nipples, skillfully rolling and applying pressure.

The drinks are making me brave. "Honey, I want to play rough tonight. I want to get spanked in these panties," I murmur against his lips.

"I sense you have something to show me, Baby. Lift your arms in the air, Katarina," he instructs. I do as he asks, and he effortlessly slides the gown over my head and throws it on the couch. "You are breathtakingly beautiful," he says, continuing his exploration around my now bare nipples, rolling and gently squeezing before tracing patterns across my stomach and down to my panties. "I want you to turn around so I can see what it is that you want to show me," he says. I feel myself moistening at the sound of his voice and begin to spin slowly.

I hear the slight intake of breath and know he's pleased. "Katarina, I love these," he murmurs as he slowly traces the curve of my hips and ass. "Bend over and hold onto the couch," he orders huskily.

Oh, God, this is hot. I lean over as far as I can and position my palms on the sofa.

He runs his hands along the thong, exploring all the way down to the seam; gently stroking my ass and hips. "Are these the panties you want to get spanked in, Baby?" he asks.

"Yes," I pant.

"And you think these sweet little panties are going to persuade me to spank you?" he asks.

"I hope so," I murmur, unable to keep the breathiness out of my voice.

"Spread your legs wide apart, Baby," he urges huskily.

"There you go," he encourages as I spread my legs as far as I can. "I think I might have misjudged your negotiation skills, Katarina. I was going to make you wait a little while longer, but I have to admit you are making it pretty difficult to resist."

The muscles in my legs, thighs, arms, and hips are starting to ache and adding to the intensity of my desire. He gently pulls on the seam of my thong, knowingly causing it to rub against my clit, and I moan softly.

"Please, Honey," I moan as he pulls the material tighter against the overly sensitive area. As I pull back, his hand smacks the right side of my ass cheek.

"Is that what you want, Katarina?" he asks.

"Yes," I pant as his hand lands on the other side of my ass, briefly rubbing the spot before landing once more dead center. Oh... I can feel that push against the special place deep inside of me, moaning as he slowly pushes a finger inside of me.

"You are dripping wet, Baby," he says as he repeats the pattern; left, right and then center, coming down hard each time, then slowly pushing two fingers inside of me.

I hear myself moan softly as he starts the third cycle. "Is this what you wanted, Baby?" he asks.

"Yes," I moan as he puts his fingers back inside of me. I try to push back, but my muscles are shaking from being in this position. I feel his hand connect with the left side of my ass, right side and then back to the center where all of my nerve endings are ready to explode. He pulls the thong aside, and with one thrust, his cock plunges deep inside of me. I gasp at the depth and intensity and feel myself clench around him.

"How does that feel, Baby?"

"Good Honey... so good," I moan.

"Baby, I want to fuck you hard. Are you ready?" he asks urgently.

"Yes," I cry out unable to stand the pressure anymore.

"Cum for me Baby, cum..." he urges, and that's it... I am lost, shaking and trembling as he plunges into my overly sensitive body, over and over, prolonging my climax while finding his own release deep inside of me. I am still quivering as he pulls me back against him, wrapping me up in his powerful arms.

"Are you feeling better now?" he asks, still holding me tightly against him.

"Well, except for a sore ass, yes," I retort, joking.

"I do believe it was quite well negotiated for, and thoroughly deserved if I recall," he admonishes. "Now, let's get you into the shower," he says, scooping me into his arms. He soaps the loofah and washes every inch of my body, circling in slow motions as I luxuriate in the feel, before soaping himself. He finishes and gets out of the shower before I've conditioned my hair. I rinse it, one last time, dry off and slide into my robe to go in search of him.

"I don't care what the fuck the government is paying. There is not going to be a negotiation about how the employees are treated in any company that is funded by me." There's a brief pause, then he continues. "You do that, pack up our teams and get the hell out of there. Shut it down, Sid," he says. As he comes out of his office, he sees me sitting on the couch.

"Things are not going so well?" I ask.

"You could say that," he says.

"How long have you been out here?" he asks cautiously.

"Long enough to hear that negotiations aren't going so well. That's twice in one night," I say, trying to lighten the mood. That does the trick; he's grinning from ear to ear and comes to sit by me.

I hand him a glass of wine, and he visibly relaxes next to me. I wonder what happened that made him pull out even after sending another team over, but don't push.

"I'm going to let Jay know that we're working at Prestian tomorrow and that we'll be heading home tomorrow night. I'll give Gaby a call and let her know we're coming in early and will stay through the weekend."

"I can work on the simulation from anywhere. I'm hoping by early next week, Terry will have a footprint set so we can start putting the user groups together. I'll be working quite a few hours once they start," I warn.

"I see the jaw clench and deepening of his eyes, a sure sign that he is not happy with the answer. "Katarina, that's why there are other people to assist you, so you don't have to work as many hours," he states.

"Chase, there are going to be times when I need to work a little longer. There is a lot to do with this project and need I remind you that you are paying me to do this?" I ask, wishing I knew why he has such an aversion to me working.

"In case you forgot, it would be quite easy to renegotiate your contract and don't think that I won't," he threatens.

"Has anyone every told you how insufferable you can sometimes be," I exclaim. "Seriously," I fume.

He laughs. "In fact... yes, I believe it was you that last called me insufferable," he states with a grin.

"I am serious, and you are making fun. I've got lots to do and want it to be done well. Why can't you understand that I enjoy my work?"

"Katarina, you're such a mystery in so many ways. The ladies I've known previously would like nothing more than not to work. I'm pleased you enjoy your job, but I don't want to see you work your life away and never have a chance to enjoy it."

"I know that Chase, and I appreciate your concern, but this project will make a difference in people's lives. I also don't want your employees to think I am handing over my job to other people and lollygagging. I'd like for them to get to know the hard-working kind of person that I am."

"Allow your team to support you and you will be able to produce much more and, as a result, have a much better work-life balance. I learned that years ago but didn't know about the theory of constraints at the time. Mary said you approved of Renee as your assistant. She has been with the company quite some time, and has a lot of untapped potential."

I yawn, and it does not go unnoticed. He scoops me up gently, kissing me on the forehead as he carries me through the suite and places me on the king-size bed. I wiggle out of the robe and slip underneath the goose down covers while he is in the bathroom, thinking about how I can make him understand how I feel, but I am overcome by the long day and fall asleep.

THREE

In the morning, I shower and set out to find Chase. By this time he has usually gotten his workout in, and is already eating breakfast. I can't find him so I decide to text him.

Message: Where are you?

Reply: At work.

Message: I thought the plan was to head in together. It's only 7 a.m.

Reply: Text Jay when you're ready.

Message: Are you okay? Why did you leave without me?

Reply: Get some breakfast. I'll call you shortly.

Is he mad about me working? Jeez!

Going through the closet, I make a mental note to do some clothes shopping so I can leave some here as well as at the house. I text Jay to let him know I am ready to go.

Message: Okay. We're going to need about 10 minutes. I'll text you when we're clear.

Reply: Clear?

Message: Clear.

I'm puzzled, but take the few minutes to have a banana. My phone rings and I answer Chase's ringtone.

"Katarina, I don't have a lot of time to talk, but we've had a lot of backlash from pulling out of the overseas deal. Security is being tightened for everyone. Jay will be up shortly to escort you to work, and he'll have a couple other members of his team with him. They will be assigned to you going forward. I'll fill you in when you get here," he says.

"Okay," I say, wondering what could have happened.

"What, no arguments this morning?" he asks.

"No, I told you I am going to try to leave things up to you," I say.

"Good, I'll see you when you get here," he says, and I think I hear the relief in his voice before he hangs up.

The knock sounds a few seconds later, and I open the door to find Jay standing there with two men. "Kate you remember Sheldon and Derek from Aruba," he says. They extend their hands to greet me with a "nice to see you again ma'am," making me at once feel older than my twenty-six years.

"Come in," I say, inviting the men into the foyer. Jay closes the door behind them.

"We're going to have to go over a few things, Kate. First, I need you to put both Sheldon and Derek's numbers in your phone contacts. They already have yours," he says.

"Right now?" I ask, my eyes rising in question.

"Sorry Kate. I know you're not a big fan of all the security, but we've got orders from Chase."

"It's okay, Jay," I state reassuringly.

They each give me their numbers, and I enter them into my contacts. "Also, if you can give us about a ten-minute window before you want to go anywhere, that will allow us enough time to secure the vehicles. I'll let Chase explain the rest of it to you," he says.

"Thanks, Jay," I say, knowing that it won't help to express my frustration to him.

I'm escorted to the car, and Jay introduces me to Matt, another member of security, who gets out of the driver's seat as Jay opens the rear passenger door for me. Dereck slides into the front, and Jay takes the driver's seat.

"Be right behind you," Matt says to Jay as he and Sheldon walk away. I'm in the backseat taking all this in. *This is serious. What the hell happened that made Chase raise my security to this level*, I wonder.

As we pull to a stop, Dereck quickly gets out of the front and holds the door open for me. Matt arrives and trades places with Jay. Clearly no valet today. I give the bellman an apologetic smile as we go into the building. The elevators open and Jay grasps my shoulder lightly to keep me from entering. "Kate, we'll take the next one," he says as Dereck gets into the elevator heading up. He briefly looks at his phone and then allows us to use the next one. We reach our floor and Dereck and Jay both walk in with me.

I stop to talk with Mary a few moments, and she lets me know Chase is awaiting my arrival. As we enter his office, he waves us to the chairs, listening to someone on the phone.

"Thanks, Sid. Keep me posted," he says. His eyes capture mine across the desk, and he looks tired. I wonder how much sleep he's had and suddenly long to put my arms around him.

"Good to see you again, Dereck," he says, finishing the call and standing to exchange handshakes.

"Good to be stateside, Chase," he says.

"When do the teams arrive back?" Chase asks Jay.

"We've got one group en route, but we've had difficulty locating the second team, so the pilot's been instructed to land until we determine if we need him to turn around and extract them. We have another jet on standby waiting for Sid and his team," he says hesitantly, briefly glancing at me.

"I haven't filled Katarina in yet, Jay, but you can talk in front of her. She was asleep when I left. Otherwise, I would have briefed her," Chase says.

"Chase, the protestors have surrounded the building. I just talked with Sid, and he believes they are poised for more rioting. He's working with the local facility team to see if they will intervene since the demonstrators are protesting both their government and us, for not moving forward with the project. They need work desperately in that area of the country," Jay explains.

"Keep the second team on reserve, but let's hope we can persuade the facility men to intervene. If not, we'll need to send them in. How are their supplies?" Chase asks.

"Food and water supplies are fine, and they just received an ammunition supply a few days ago, so well stocked," Jay says. My eyes lift in surprise. *What in the world are they doing,* I think to myself.

"Keep me posted and thank you both for bringing Katarina in today," he says, rising to see them out.

"I'll text you with plans later," he says to Jay shutting the door behind him. He sits back in his chair, watching me intently for a few moments, and I see a mix of emotions play out in his eyes.

"You look so tired. How much sleep did you get last night? I ask.

"Not much," he admits. "I had a lot on my mind and then all hell broke loose," he says.

"What happened, exactly?" I ask.

"The locals learned we were planning to pull out, and are rioting. I'm not going to allow the mistreatment of women, or anyone, for that matter, in any plant that has the Prestian name on it. The government thinks we are interfering in their culture and beliefs, which of course we are. They couldn't come to terms with the labor clause of the contract so we're at an impasse.

I told Sid to pull out and the locals are furious with our company and their local government: they need the work to survive. The citizens were in full swing last night and started rioting; fires erupted close to one of the refineries, and a lot of people were severely injured. They are not sure, yet, if it was intentionally set or just an accident as a result of carelessness. The rioters seem to have settled down this morning, but another group of protestors has surrounded city center where Sid and his team are. We're hoping they don't start rioting again and that we can get them out without violence," he explains.

"That's why I have more security. You think I am in danger because of this?" I ask.

"Katarina, I'm not prepared to take the risk. These people have far-reaching arms, and many that are sympathetic to their beliefs live right here in our own backyard. As of last night, every member of our family's security level was increased. Katarina, we are going to need to talk to your mom," he says.

"You think my mom is at risk?" I gasp.

"Baby, I am not willing to take a chance with someone that means so much to you. There is already a team watching her, but we really need to bring her up to speed in a couple different respects," he explains.

"You flew a team to Naples to watch my mom?" I ask incredulously.

He raises his eyebrows as if the answer is obvious. "Katarina, I believe you said you were going to start letting me handle things. In fact, promises were made in this area. I was planning to surprise you with a trip to Naples on Friday. I thought you might like to spend some time together which would allow me to learn more about your dad, but given the situation, we're going to need to make the trip today."

"Chase we can't just show up and tell my mom she needs round the clock security. She will absolutely flip," I exclaim.

"Would you please stop worrying? Why don't you call your mom and tell her we're going to be in town tonight and would like to take her out to dinner. She typically leaves work around four thirty and goes to the gym. According to the security report she usually stops by the supermarket for meat and produce, and typically arrives home around six thirty. I've made reservations at Bay Shore at seven p.m. We can have dinner and get to know each other a little better. Why don't you have her meet us there," he suggests.

I'm stunned that he knows so much about my mom and already has everything planned. "Chase, I don't know what to say. Thank you for thinking of my mom, but you're sure it's necessary for her to have security, too?"

"You're welcome, and unfortunately, it is, Katarina," he says, brushing my hair out of my face and kissing me on the mouth. "Why don't you go to your office, call your mom and let her know we're coming? Renee has moved into the vacant space adjacent to yours. You might want to leave her with things she can do in our absence. I'm not sure when we'll be back into the office after today."

"What time are we leaving?" I ask, trying to comprehend everything that's happening.

"It's about a two and a half hour flight. We'll take the helicopter from here to the airport and avoid the city traffic, but we should still leave around three thirty this afternoon," he says.

I walk out of his office and see Matt standing by the elevator as I head for the executive suites. As I round the corner, I'm surprised to see Dereck at one of the collaborative workstations, most often utilized by administrators who need space in between meetings with people in the building. He fits right in today wearing a dark suit, light shirt and conservative tie.

I smile as I pass him on the way to Renee's office. She is seated behind the desk and stands when I walk in. "You must be Renee. I've heard so many good things about you and am happy you accepted the offer to work on the Prestian Medical Center project," I say, shaking her hand.

"Thank you very much, Miss Meilers. I am excited about the opportunity," she says.

"Please, call me Kate."

"Okay, I will," she says warmly.

Chase just informed me that we may not be here much of next week. I need to make a phone call, but after that, if you want to we can spend some time going over things for next week," I offer.

"That sounds perfect. Just let me know when you are ready."

I close my office door and settle in to call my mom. I have no idea how to start this conversation. She's at work, hopefully not in a meeting. "Siri, call Mom," I say, settling into my chair.

"Hi Sweetheart," she says. I can hear the surprise in her voice. I never call during the day.

"Hi, Mom."

"I haven't heard from you in a little while. I thought you might be working long hours so was going to try you over the weekend," she explains.

I know she must be wondering why it took me so long to call her, after all she told me at the hospital. "It looks like we can catch up a little sooner than that. Chase and I are going to be in Naples tonight," I explain.

"You're kidding? You're coming here, tonight?" she asks. She sounds excited, and my heart catches a little... I feel horrible that I've only responded to her texts and not called to talk with her since our conversation at the hospital.

"He made reservations at a place called Bay Shore for seven o'clock. Can we meet you there?" I ask.

"Absolutely. It's a charming restaurant. I can't wait to see you," she says.

"I'm looking forward to seeing you too, Mom. I love you," I say, wishing that we didn't have to bring her bad news.

"Love you too, Sweetie," she says before hanging up.

Well, that wasn't so bad.

Message: Talked to Mom and she'll meet us at 7.

Reply: Go okay?

Message: Yes, she sounded excited to see us.

I find Renee and soon become immersed in workflows and diagrams. I have already sent Terry some of them, but explain each of them to her and why they are used. "I haven't moved any of my books from my office at Torzial. If I had them here, you could read them while I'm gone."

"Kate, we have delivery associates. I can arrange to have them picked up from Torzial if you have someone pick out the books you're referring to," she offers.

"Good idea, Renee. I'll arrange for someone to leave them at the front desk." I turn and see Chase lounging in the doorway.

"Are you ladies going to work right through lunch or would you like to go out for a bite?" he asks.

"Thanks for the offer and for approving my new position, Mr. Prestian, but my boyfriend should be here momentarily. He's taking me out to celebrate," she says, smiling.

"You're most welcome, Renee. Maybe another time then. Enjoy your lunch," he says before we leave to walk the short distance to a local restaurant. The amount of security we have with us is unnerving.

Sheldon and Matt take the lead, walking towards the entrance. I don't glance back, but know without a doubt Jay and Dereck are pulling up the rear. We walk the short distance back to Prestian from lunch, and as is becoming routine, Matt and Sheldon take the elevator up first. Jay looks at his phone and gives Chase the nod... he knows we're clear and will be taking the next one. Dereck and Jay escort us up and Dereck heads back to the collaborative workstation which is centrally located. Chase places his hand on the small of my back leading me to the executive suites. As we get closer, Matt comes out of my office. He gives Chase the nod as he passes by, and I know he's making sure it is secure. *What the hell.* We walk into my office, and I shut the door this time.

"Chase, is there something else you are not telling me? You seriously have them checking the entire floor? How do you think someone is going to get past security when we haven't even been gone but for an hour?"

"Katarina, I know the security stuff is hard for you to get used to, but it's essential right now," he says. "I get taking precautions, but this is like James Bond shit for crying out loud," I exclaim.

He captures my lips with his own, effectively sealing off any further argument, kissing me deeply. "Baby, I am not about to take any chances with you. Things are escalating for Sid and in all likelihood, they will do whatever they can to make Prestian Corp, mainly me, see things their way," he explains.

"I'm sorry, Chase. I know you are just trying to protect us, but I'm scared," I admit.

"Katarina, I contemplated not telling you but decided to inform you so you had a heightened awareness of the situation. I'm sorry you're frightened, but we have the best security money can buy. Jay's team is not about to let anything happen to us Baby, but it means things will be tightened significantly. You're going to need to run inside for a little while, Katarina. It won't last long, but we need to get through the next couple weeks," he says. He is watching me warily, and I know he is waiting for my reaction.

He looks so tired, he's clearly been up most of the night, and we still have a full flight to Florida and night with my mom to get through. I suddenly have an overwhelming desire just to please him. "I guess I'll have to beat you to the treadmill each morning," I say.

"Thank you, Baby."

I reach up, stroking the back of his neck with my hands, bending his head down towards me. I claim his lips with mine; gently exploring, my tongue finding its way and I feel his hardness as he pulls me tight against him.

He lets me go briefly to lock the door, pushing the button that brings the privacy blinds into place. "I want you now, Katarina," he says. His eyes are molten, and I moisten at the sheer carnal intent I see reflected in his eyes.

"What about the in the air experience you promised me?" I ask hoarsely.

"Oh, Baby, you will get that, too," he promises, pulling me toward him.

"I want to fuck you over your desk. Now be a good girl and bend over," he coaxes. I lean over my desk and feel his hands pushing my dress up past my waist. He slides my panties over my hips, leisurely, allowing his hands to glide over my curves as he pulls them down to my ankles. I hear his zipper come down and anticipate the feel of his cock.

"Baby, you are so wet and ready for me," he says, rubbing his length against my moistness. He pushes the head of his cock inside of me, slowly, teasing me and then suddenly plunges in, filling me. He does not move, and the fullness is unbearable. I attempt to grind shamelessly against him, but he holds me still. Feel me, Baby," he says into my ear.

"Honey," I moan, as I feel the length of his cock inside of me. It's so deep this way, and I feel myself building and then he begins sliding over that spot, over and over... I push back against him, meeting him, taking him in as far as I can as my body spirals out of control.

"Cum for me, Baby," he moans, and I lose myself as he pounds into me, prolonging my orgasm while releasing deep inside of me. We slowly catch our breath, holding each other tight as we come down from our high. He gently eases out of me, and hands me some tissue.

"Good thing my office was designed with a bathroom and shower for just the occasion," I say.

"Indeed, it was," he says, kissing me. He still looks tired, but somehow less worried.

"Feel better, now?" I ask softly.

"Just what I needed," he states wickedly, his green eyes glinting.

"Now off to the shower so we can get some work done and get in the air," he says.

"Yeah, I really haven't gotten much work done today. I spent most of my morning with Renee."

"The time you spent with her will pay off," he says, heading into the shower. He's in and out before I know it, drying off quickly. It's surreal having a shower and private bathroom in my office suite. I peel out of my clothes and jump in the shower not surprised at all to find my favorite brands, along with two loofahs. I quickly shower, dry off, let my hair down and get redressed.

He's in my reading chair, talking on the phone and his face is grim. "The teams are already on the ground and heading your way. If you think they are looking to restart negotiations, I'm willing to keep them on standby, but if we don't receive an immediate yes, I'm sending them in before this escalates and you and the team get stuck. Give me a call-back, and Sid, be careful," he says, disconnecting and immediately pressing another contact. "Jay, Chase here. Hold the teams in place. Sid is going to continue negotiations. He doesn't think they expected us to pull out over the labor issues. He wants a little time and is going to work another angle. I'll be in touch. Thanks, Jay," he says.

"Baby, I'm going to need to go back to my office and get a few things done before we leave. Try to finish up anything here that you can't do remotely. I'll stop by when we're ready to go," he says, kissing me firmly on the mouth.

FOUR

To: <u>TPartes@Martel&Sons.org</u>
   From: <u>KMeilers@TorzialConsulting.org</u>
   CC: <u>CHPrestian@PrestianCorp.org</u>,
   <u>JWarling@TorzialConsulting.org</u>

HI TERRY,

I've seen the emails from the physician groups concerned over the number of exam rooms called for in the plan. I'm running their historical and projected visit volume and will use that for the simulation demonstration. Please do not feel the need to spend any additional time drawing alternates. I believe once they have seen the simulation and understand how the office hours have been load leveled, they will be comfortable with fewer exams. Also, let me know if you would like to sit in on the simulation.

Thanks,

KATE

Kate Meilers

Project Consultant
Torzial Consulting Firm

TO: <u>KMeilers@TorzialConsulting.org</u>
   From: <u>CHPrestian@PrestianCorp.org</u>

I'M PLANNING to attend the simulation demonstration. I'd like to see how it works. Let me know when it's scheduled so Mary can rearrange my schedule. Are you almost ready?

C. **H. Prestian**
   Chief Executive Officer, Owner
   Prestian Corporation

TO: <u>CHPrestian@PrestianCorp.org</u>
   From: <u>KMeilers@TorzialConsulting.org</u>

I'M READY.

KATE

KATE MEILERS
   Project Consultant
   Torzial Consulting Firm

TO: <u>KMeilers@TorzialConsulting.org</u>
  From: <u>CHPrestian@PrestianCorp.org</u>

GOOD! I'll be there shortly.

C. **H. Prestian**
  Chief Executive Officer, Owner
  Prestian Corporation

AS GOOD AS his word Chase is in the doorway, just as I'm finishing the last of my emails. As I pack up my Mac, he answers his phone. "Chase, here. Is everything in place? Yes, we can do that. No, it'll be very late. I'll text you when we leave Naples," he says.

He guides me through the administrative suites to the elevator and pushes the code for the rooftop. Matt takes the first elevator, and Jay and Dereck take the next one up with us to the helicopter pad. "Here, put these ear plugs in and don't take them out until we land," he says to me.

I put them in, and then don the headset he hands me, glad for the extra protection against the noise. The flight from Prestian to the airport is less than ten minutes and would have taken us forty-five minutes by car. I recognize the Prestian emblem on the Gulfstream waiting for us on the strip and abundance of guards who have secured the plane. Chase takes my hand; steadying me as we board the jet, shaking hands with the captain and crew, before leading me toward the plush leather loveseat that faces a brick covered fireplace.

Jay, Dereck, Matt, and Sheldon join us taking seats in the recliners by the windows, and I realize they are coming with us to meet my mom. Chase looks down at his phone and texts someone a message.

"Everything's in place for tonight, Chase. Brian flew down ahead of us with his team, and they have the transportation and restaurant covered," Jay says.

"Thanks, Jay," Chase says. I'm sure the look of shock is on my face. An entirely different team is working to make sure we have security at the restaurant. The captain makes the announcement that we are ready for take-off, and we're soon plummeting down the runway. Once we're airborne Chase unfastens his seatbelt and undoes mine for me.

"Let's rest while we have a chance," he says, leading me towards the bedroom suite at the back of the plane. He locks the door, discarding his suit jacket and tie, laying them across the back of one of the chairs next to the bar area.

"I'm going to have a drink, would you like one?" he asks. I notice the bottle has already been opened; he's apparently planned ahead.

"Yes, please." I slip my sandals off and run my toes through the luxurious carpet. It feels heavenly, smooth as silk. I look up and catch him smiling. He sits next to me and takes my hand.

"Do you want to take the lead in telling your mom about the security issues and discussing the details of your father, Katarina?"

"I'm not sure if I've had enough time to absorb everything she told me about my dad, yet, and honestly don't know how she's going to react to the security situation," I say.

"She needs to know about the current circumstances, and I need to know about your dad," he says, watching my reaction warily.

"Why don't you just handle it?" I ask, taking him by surprise. His expression, usually well controlled, registers the shock on his face.

"Katarina, that's a big step. I know how nervous you are about this. Are you positive? If left up to me, I am going to be very honest and upfront with your mom," he warns.

"Chase, you always think I don't trust you. I do. I am just scared. Look at everything you are doing to protect my mom. I can't believe how much logistically had to happen to make the trip possible. I trust you with my life," I say, hoping to ease some of the worries from his tired face.

"You couldn't have made me happier, Katarina," he says, pulling me into his arms. "Now, I think someone promised me a little mile-high action tonight," he says, looking down at me with those intense eyes.

"Chase, I thought you were tired!"

"Baby, I'm never that tired. Now, let me help you out of this dress..."

I am thoroughly exhausted after another round of lovemaking, slow, and unhurried this time. "Baby, get some rest, and I'll wake you before we land," he says, kissing me on the forehead.

"Why don't you curl up with me and take a nap?" I ask, not wanting to lose the feel of his body next to mine.

"As good as that sounds, I have things to do before we land. Maybe on the way back," he says, getting out of bed to dress.

"That reminds me, are we really flying home after we meet with mom?" I ask.

"Yes, It will be late, but I want us to be back home tonight. We're going to stay there until the worst of this is over. Security is making preparations as we speak and Gaby is aware," he says, leaning down to kiss me before he leaves the cabin.

I stir a little while later to a gentle nudging. "Katarina, wake up and get dressed, Baby. We're going to land shortly. We need to take our seats before long, captain's orders," he teases.

I glance at the clock on my phone. What a difference an hour of rest can make. I wish Chase had been able to sleep. I slip back into my clothes and go to the bathroom to freshen up. All my brands... I brush my teeth and notice the long white terry cloth robe hanging from the hook. *One at every place he owns.* I freshen up my makeup and brush my hair, which for some reason doesn't seem too unruly tonight. I grab my purse and decide to stay barefoot, carrying my sandals instead of wearing them. Chase is not far behind me and slides into his seat, just as I am fastening my seatbelt. He smiles widely when he notices my bare feet. "What?" I ask smiling.

He shakes his head bemused. "Later," he says. The plane lands perfectly. Dereck and Matt lead us towards one of the largest stretch limos I have ever seen. Jay and Sheldon are right behind us. The magnitude of his wealth is incomprehensible to me. I am ushered into the back seat, and Chase slides in beside me before the crew enters. The limousine is equipped with two mini bars, overhead televisions, and iPads installed in front of each seat.

"Keith, it's good to see you," Chase says to the driver. "Thanks for making the trip out with your team."

"Anytime Chase. We are in good position, and the restaurant has been checked by security. The hostess has instructions so when you arrive she'll escort you to the table."

Jay leans over to me from the opposite seat. "You'll have to text Chase or me if you need to go to the bathroom. We have female detail deployed at the restaurant if that should happen," he says. *Are you fucking kidding me*, I almost say out loud.

Chase squeezes my hand reassuringly and leans over so only I can hear, "Baby, play nice. They are a little on edge because we are in different territory. At home, they know every nook and cranny... but here," he shrugs. We head to Bay Shore in relative silence, and as we pull up, Jay instructs the team and Chase.

True to his word the hostess knows exactly where to seat everyone. Chase and I are at a table, overlooking the water, with room for two more diners; Jay and Sheldon have one table, Matt and Dereck have another and Keith is outside. I don't know how many more people in the restaurant are part of Jay's team.

The waitress asks if she can bring us anything while we wait for our party, and Chase orders a bottle of white wine, letting the server know when the last member of our party arrives we'll want a glass of the finest sweet red.

"You know what my mom drinks?" I ask, scanning my recollection about conversations we've had and not recalling any that discussed her preference for wines.

"Katarina, I had a team assigned to record her activity in the event we ever needed to protect her. She goes to the grocery store, and red wine is sometimes on her list, but never white. Likewise, when she goes out with clients, she most often has a glass of red wine with her meal. I'm sorry it's disturbing to you, but it's essential to the security detail," he says. His expression is determined and gives nothing away.

I am about to reply when my mom enters the door. I scowl at him instead. This is really too much. My mom spots us immediately and says something to the hostess, who escorts her to our table. I throw my arms around my mom hugging her close to me.

It's so good to see you, Sweetheart," she exclaims, squeezing me tightly.

Chase rises, and my mom is quick to hug him, too. "Chase, good to see you again, and this time under better circumstances," she says as Chase pulls her chair out for her.

"Karissa, Katarina and I were just enjoying a glass of white wine. I understand you like a sweet red, so took the liberty of ordering; it should be out momentarily," he says. I squint my eyes at him to let him know that we are not through with this conversation.

"Thank you, Chase," a glass of wine sounds lovely. "How was the traffic from the airport?" she asks.

"It was pretty quiet compared to the Chicago traffic," I answer truthfully as the waitress arrives with her wine.

"Karissa, have you been to this restaurant before? It seemed to have great reviews, so I hope it's okay," he says politely. I admire his ability to command a conversation and put everyone at ease.

"I've been here several times with clients. The food and atmosphere have always been superb, and the view of the water is such an advantage. Surprisingly, there are very few restaurants on the water in Naples. They serve fresh gulf-water fish and shellfish. One of their specialties is the grilled grouper with lemon sauce. It's excellent, as are the seared bay scallops," she says.

The waitress comes back, and Chase orders an appetizer tray of shrimp, crab, oysters and calamari before the waiter asks for our entrée selections.

Mom and I order a blackened grouper salad the waitress recommends which comes with a creamy dill dressing. "I'll have the grilled grouper with lemon sauce. It comes highly recommended," he says, smiling at the waitress and winning points with my mom.

The appetizers arrive, and Chase asks questions of my mom allowing her to regale us with stories about the area. I am nervous and have already finished my glass of wine. Chase requests another glass of wine for my mom and pours me one from the bottle on the table. I wonder if he thinks that I need to relax. I notice he has not even finished half of his first glass.

"So, what brought you kids to town? Katie called me this morning to tell me you were coming, but we didn't talk long," my mom says.

Chase captures my eyes with his... one more chance they seem to say... I nod.

"Well, in all honesty, I was planning to bring Katarina to Naples on Friday and spend the weekend getting to know you a little better, but one of my projects took an unexpected turn that changed our plans. Prestian Corp is working on a contract to rebuild an overseas plant. It would bring a lot of jobs to the area, and at the same time allow our government better position politically and technologically, which is why we are willing to fund it. Unfortunately, there has been some upheaval in the region. In light of the recent activity, I am taking extra precautions with members of my family, Katarina, and her family. We wanted to tell you in person and didn't wish to wait until the weekend," he says.

I am awestruck by his ability to summarize the situation so concisely and honestly for my mom.

"Are you telling me that my daughter is in danger?" she asks, eyeing him warily.

"Karissa, I will not let harm come to her or anyone she loves which is why I have a large security team watching her and you around the clock," he says.

She audibly gasps. "What?" she asks, looking at me for something.

"Mom, it's just a precaution. The security teams are excellent, and I love that Chase thought of your safety right away," I say in hopes of alleviating her concern.

"Chase, you might need to order me a bottle of this wine," she exclaims.

"I think that can be arranged," he says, catching the waitress's attention with a flip of his hand. "I took the liberty of putting a security detail in place for you last night and wanted to make you aware as quickly as we could. I didn't want you to inadvertently realize you were being followed and get scared."

"I see," she says, seemingly sizing up the situation. But I know my mom. She is never speechless.

"Karissa, you are safer than you ever have been, as is your daughter.

I can assure you the highest levels of security are in place, and I don't think it will last long. The region is dying, and they need this plant. I am unwilling to negotiate treatment of the employees in the facility which is a source of contention for them. If the government can work through their cultural barriers, I think an agreement may be forthcoming in the next week or so. We need to be prepared that some sympathizers may retaliate if given a chance. I don't intend to provide them with the opportunity."

"So, what does this security involve?" she asks.

"We currently have a full team stationed in Naples. They know your daily routines so have been trying to stay a step ahead of you, but we need to develop a plan for how we proceed. There are two options, Karissa. Stay in Naples with a security team assigned or fly back to Chicago with Katarina and me tonight. If you decide to stay here, I will introduce you to Keith, who I would assign as your security lead. He has worked for the family for years and is completely trustworthy. He will want to know exactly where you are going and when. If you fly to Chicago tonight, you can stay with us in our home outside of the city. Katarina and I will be working from home for the next couple of weeks, and I assure you security is impeccable. You can think of it as a vacation. I would prefer this option, so Katarina is not worried about you. It would also give us a chance to get to know each other better and for you and Katarina to catch up."

My mom is visibly taken aback. "You mean like tonight," she says incredulously, glaring at me like I could have given her some warning.

I shrug. "It's a lovely home, Mom, and you can work from there... easily. There is plenty of room, and it would be fun to catch up."

`"I just need time to think about this. If I stay here, someone will follow me to work and back every day?" she asks.

Chase intervenes. "If you decide to stay here, they will not only follow you to and from work but will guard you at your place of employment. You will notify them of every move you are going to make at least ten minutes before you do so they can clear the area. I'm not about to risk someone that Katarina cares so greatly about. Like I said, coming home with us tonight would be the preferred option, but I understand if you need to stay," he says.

"You really have plenty of room for me for a couple of weeks?" she asks.

"Mom, we have plenty of room," I say.

"I would need my computer for work," she says, tentatively.

"Karissa, do you access things from the net or your hard drive? We have spare Macs at home," Chase says.

"Well, I could, but I have a lot of documents saved on my computer."

"Very well, do you have a key or combination? If so, Keith's team can go get your computer while we finish dinner," he says.

"You're kidding," she says, clearly taken aback.

"I seldom kid, Karissa, and am not joking now. I would prefer, given the situation and time of night, they procure it for you. Do you have any personal belongings you must have, or can we buy you a couple of weeks' worth of clothes?" he asks.

"You are completely serious, aren't you?" she asks.

"I am Karissa; in fact, it would please me very much if you let Keith and his teams go get your computer while we finish our meal. We can arrange to have clothing brought to the house before we arrive."

"I'm clearly in over my head," she says, frowning at me.

Welcome to my world.

"She reaches into her purse and brings out a magnetic key card and another set of keys. "They will need this to enter the building and then this for the door to my office. When you get off the third floor..."

"They know their way, Karissa. Don't worry," he says and is on his phone texting. Shortly someone I have not met stops by the table.

"We'll meet you on the plane," Chase says, giving him both keys.

I think I am in shock. My mom is coming home with us. Unbelievable! I reach for my phone, and all I can think to do is text Chase Mom's size.

Message: Mom is a size 8

Reply: They know...Her clothes will arrive before she does.

"What should we do with my car?" my mom asks.

"We'll have someone drive it back to your home and park it in the garage," he says.

She doesn't ask how he knows she has a garage but gives me a "what the hell" type of a look.

"Karissa, they'll let us know when they have procured your laptop. I feel much better knowing you'll be coming back with us. There are a few things, though, we still need to discuss. I need to know about Katarina's father. I will keep the information completely confidential, but I need to know who he is so I can put security precautions in place. Rest assured, your safety, as well as Katarina's, will be my utmost concern. I've taken the liberty of doing some preliminary research, and based on what we already know, I think Katarina's dad is Carlos Larussio, but I need you to confirm this, Karissa," he says.

She audibly gasps. "I'm not sure how you found his identity with what I told Katarina, but her dad is Carlos Larussio," she admits, looking from me to Chase in shock and disbelief.

"Thank you, Karissa. The families are based out of New York and are friends of my family," he says.

I look up in surprise. "Oh, dear Lord," she says, clearly distressed with his revelation.

"Karissa, it's not what you think. While the family may have a history, they are also involved in many very legitimate and lucrative business ventures. Some of which happen to be with members of my family and myself," he adds, pausing to gauge her reaction.

"I see," is all she says. It is hard for me to know what she's thinking or how she is feeling. I have never seen her at such a loss for words before.

"Mom, it will be okay," I assure, taking her hand in mine.

Chase looks down at his phone. "Ladies we've got the all clear. Shall we go?" he asks, seemingly more relaxed than before we arrived. I realize it's because he knows everyone will be safe. One less thing to worry about, I'm sure. As we stand, I notice Matt and Dereck at the table in front of us, do likewise and take the lead. We follow them, and I'm positive without looking that Jay and Sheldon are bringing up the rear. Matt and Dereck lead us to the limo and open the doors for us. Chase helps my mother and me into the back seat and then slides in next to me. It's a half-hour ride to the airport, and everyone is relatively quiet. Chase has his arm protectively around me. Jay gives us an update that they retrieved Mom's computer, and it's on its way to the plane.

Chase's phone rings and he answers it immediately. "No, we're on our way to the airport. We have Katarina's mom with us. She'll stay at our home until things clear over. Emily's family all moved in? Good, I'll give you a quick call when we're home. Love you, too." he says before disconnecting.

I suddenly realize the enormity of all that Chase has been dealing with since last night. He has been moving everyone his family cares about into protection. My heart swells with the love I feel for this man. Why can't I tell him I love him? *Is it true I don't trust him with my emotions?*

FIVE

We reach the airport, and the limo pulls up as close as it can to the jet. Chase escorts us through the plane door and talks to the crew for a few moments while everyone gets settled in. He drops into the seat next to mine just as we finish buckling and glances at his phone. He frowns slightly and texts a message.

"Anything wrong?" I ask.

"Nothing for you to worry about, Baby," he says, taking my hand in his as we settle in for takeoff.

"This is a beautiful airplane. It's a little different than the one you flew me to Chicago in a few weeks ago, isn't it?" my mom asks Chase.

"Yes, this is a few years newer, but we had the interior done very similarly. We have several since it saves the executive team a lot of time sitting in airports and hotels," he says. Chase and my mom seem to be getting along splendidly, spending the majority of the flight getting to know each other. It is a clear night, and the flight home is smooth right down to the landing. Chase reaches into his pockets and pulls out two sets of earplugs. "Here... we're going to take the helicopter over to the house. Put these in until we land," he instructs, handing my mom and me the plugs and then a set of headphones. My mom gives me another one of her what the hell looks, and I can only shrug. A ten-minute ride in the air is much nicer than driving through traffic. Even at this late hour, traffic in downtown Chicago can be a pain. I'm surprised how lit up the estate is as we hover and then put down precisely on the helipad. A group of men I have not met before greets us as we get out of the helicopter. Chase begins shaking hands, thanking them for their assistance and seems to be on a first-name basis with everyone. Gaby swings the door open wide to greet us as we reach the house.

Chase introduces my mother to Gaby. "I'm very pleased to meet you, Karissa. I have one of the guest suites prepared for you, and your clothes are in the closet. If you need anything else, please let me know," Gaby says warmly.

"Thank you very much," my mom says.

Would you ladies care for a glass of wine?" Chase asks. It's late, but I realize now he probably wasn't comfortable drinking until he knew we were safely home.

"Sure, I'll have a glass with you. It'll probably put me to sleep, though," I admit, trying to suppress a yawn.

"Mom, would you like a glass of red wine?" I ask.

"Yes, please," she says. Gaby brings out a tray of freshly baked bread, Brie, sliced pears, apples, and nuts.

Chase's phone swooshes and he reaches for it, smiles, and texts a message. I cut a couple small pieces of bread and generously spread them with brie for my mom and Chase. I look up, and Chase is smiling broadly at me. "It is excellent, Gaby," he exclaims, cutting himself another piece.

"I think I'll go to bed now that I know everyone is safely home. I made some pies for tomorrow. We'll see if they make it that long with these two around," she says to my mom, giving us a playful scowl.

"Why don't I show you to your room, Karissa and we can do the full blown tour tomorrow," Chase suggests.

"That sounds good, all the excitement and wine have gone straight to my head. I'm sure I'll be asleep the minute my head hits a pillow," she says. Chase leads the way to the other side of the house, down corridors and past rooms that I have not yet even seen. He opens a door, and we enter what appears to be a large living suite. I take note of the small kitchenette, and a sizeable living room with windows from floor to ceiling on one side and a massive fireplace on the other.

"You can work from here," he says, opening the door into an adjoining room with a large desk, Mom's computer, a large monitor and not surprisingly a big screen on the wall in the corner. As Mom and I leave the room, he is on his phone texting again.

"The guys hooked up a larger monitor for your laptop since you had it set up that way at home. The computer is authenticated with rights to our server so you can sign in with the password by your laptop. I hope you'll find everything that you need, but if not, just let me know," he says to my mom.

"I don't know what to say, Chase. I really appreciate your hospitality," she replies.

"It's a pleasure. Gaby has left coffee in your kitchen along with a few of your other favorites in the refrigerator. Please feel free to join us downstairs for breakfast. I just wanted you to have a few things in the event you wake early. I'll show you to your room and then I am going to retire myself. It's been a rather long day," he says, leading us towards the master suite which proudly displays an ornate king-size bed, another fireplace and master bathroom fully equipped with a whirlpool.

"I'll give you both a tour of the full house tomorrow. There is a gym upstairs and pool room on the lower level that you are welcome to use," he says to my mom.

"Thank you, both. I am exhausted, and the bed looks heavenly. I'll see you kids in the morning," she says.

"Good night, Mom. I'm so glad you came. It'll be fun spending a little time together," I say, giving her a hug.

Chase guides me through the suite, his hand at the small of my back until we get to the main hall, and I know where I'm going. "It's like a maze," I say.

"You'll learn your way around soon enough," he says, leading us up the elevator and to our room.

"You seem so much more relaxed, Honey," I say as we climb into bed.

"It's been a long day, and I'm glad we're home. The security team is always a little jumpy when we're off grounds when these things occur," he says.

"Chase, does this type of thing happen a lot?" I ask.

"I would not say it's common, but it is something we have to deal with from time to time. Now, I think someone wanted me to curl them up and go to sleep if I recall correctly," he says pulling me close, curling his body around mine.

I wake to sunlight pouring into the room. I glance at my phone on the side table, and it's already 10:15 a.m. I can hardly believe I slept this late. Chase is obviously already up and moving. I've missed three calls from Jenny, but she didn't leave a message, so it must not be urgent. I see she's also left a text for me.

Message: Hey, give me a call when you can.

Reply: Sorry, we were out late last night. Call me when you get a chance.

I need to go for a run and clear my head after last night's events. I select a pair of running shorts, sports bra, socks and shoes and then throw on a t-shirt not knowing who I will run into on my way to the gym. I find my way to the treadmill, pull off my t-shirt, select my playlist and turn it to shuffle. It takes me a few minutes to figure out the operations of the machine, but once I do I'm lost in the music, and my thoughts. I have to admit, while one of the downsides of running on the treadmill is usually the view, that's certainly not the case in this situation. The sprawling window overlooks the choppy blue of Lake Michigan and the trees around the property are adorned with brilliant gold, yellow, red and orange leaves. I adjust the speed, getting used to the stationary equipment and my breathing. I am reflecting on the events of the last night. I still can't believe my mom agreed to come with us and how did Chase figure out who my father was? Carlos Larussio. I say the name out loud. Chase said he was a friend of the family. What a small world. I can't help but wonder what he looks like, and what it would have been like growing up with a dad. I realize I've been on for an hour, lost in my thoughts, as my cool down song comes on. I wipe the sweat from my neck and shoulders feeling invigorated now that I'm done. Jenny's ringtone blares and I take the call.

"Kate, where have you been?" she exclaims.

"I slept in; we were up late last night. We had to make a quick trip to Florida, and my mom ended up coming home with us. It's a long story... I'll tell you over drinks."

"Well, we had a little excitement ourselves last night. We had a break-in at Torzial," she says.

"What?" I exclaim. "Were you there?" I ask.

"No, it was later in the evening. I'm not sure what they were looking for, but they left a mess. I'm glad most of your stuff was sent via delivery over to Prestian Corp. I'm sorry to say they completely ransacked your office, Kate," she says. It can't be a coincidence. I better let Chase know.

"You know the even weirder part. The silent alarm was tripped, and the police arrived shortly after the burglars left. They canvassed the area to see if anyone saw anything. A local guy was a little way down the street and couldn't really see a lot, but told the police when they came out of the building three men jumped them and put them in the backseat of a car," she exclaims.

What the hell. I wonder if our security guards were watching Torzial thinking they would look for me there. I put my t-shirt back on suddenly feeling chilled. She proceeds to give me a couple of work updates and then has to hang up to catch a web conference.

Message: Where are you?

Reply: Just got off your treadmill. We may need two. BTW... I'M MAD AT YOU!

Message: We can arrange that. Whatever for? I'm intrigued.

Reply: Keeping things from me.

Message: I see. We may need to discuss this in the bedroom so I can make you see things my way.

Reply: Don't think your prowess in bed is going to get you off the hook!

HOW DID he think I would not find out about the break-in and why didn't he tell me?" He probably didn't want you to worry.

I head towards the main level finding my way back to the dining and kitchen area. "I figured you would be wherever Gaby's food is," I tease, reaching up to kiss him firmly on the lips and finding his eyes alight with amusement at our recent texting game. Gaby smiles and discreetly turns away busying herself with pulling food out of the refrigerator for lunch.

"Have you seen my mom?" I ask.

"Yes, she was down for a late breakfast, had coffee with me and then went to get some work done. You were exhausted so I thought I would let you sleep," he says.

"What about you? Did you get a better night's sleep last night?" I ask.

"I was able to get some sleep, Katarina," he says as a mirage of emotions plays over his expression.

Gaby has laid out a feast for our lunch. "Gaby it looks fantastic. You are spoiling me rotten," I add, giving her a warm smile. The meal is delicious, consisting of chicken salad with walnuts and apples, fresh oat bread, a marinated apple cider coleslaw, and fresh blackberry pie. Chase cuts two pieces of the pie and puts one on each of our plates. Dessert first," he says wickedly, laughing at the mock astonishment and disapproval on Gaby's face. She sashays past us and out of the kitchen still lamenting over the attack on her pie.

"Chase, what happened last night at Torzial? Jenny called me and said there was a break-in and that they ransacked my office. Why didn't you tell me?"

"So this is what has you upset with me? Katarina, I didn't want to add to your worry last night when you had so much on your mind with your mom. It's been taken care of," he says, regarding me somewhat warily.

"Jenny says the men were taken down by three guys while coming out of the building."

He raises his eyebrows in genuine surprise. "How does she know that?" he asks.

"Apparently the silent alarm alerted the police, and when they were talking to people afterward, someone saw it happen. It sounds like the guy was a pretty good distance away, but he could still make out what was happening," I explain, trying to gauge his reaction.

"You know a lot about something that you weren't supposed to know anything about," he says wryly.

"Chase, do you know why they were in my office?" I ask.

He looks at me thoughtfully, and I can tell he's wrestling with emotions.

"Baby, I do know why they were in your office. Which is the exact reason you and your mom are here, and we had Torzial staked out. I told you... you are in excellent hands. You have to believe that I am not going to let anything happen to you," he says.

"You didn't answer my question. Why did they break in?" I repeat.

"Katarina, isn't it obvious? They will try to get to anyone I care about to coerce me to negotiate," he says, clearly frustrated with this line of questioning.

"When did you find out?" I continue.

"On our way back from Naples," he answers.

"The last message when we were upstairs— you smiled when you texted someone. Is that when you knew things were under control?" I ask.

"You could say that," he answers hesitantly.

"I did say that. Are you going to tell me?" I persist.

"Yes, that is when I knew the situation had been contained; they were working alone, and no other plans existed that might compromise your safety," he explains, watching me intently.

I try to absorb what he's said. How does he know they were working alone, and they had no other plans? He had Torzial staked out and his team accosted the men that broke into my office.

"Is there anything else you wish to know, Katarina?" he asks, his gaze penetrating mine with his own.

"I think that's enough. I don't know how to feel about everything that's happened. I don't even want to know what laws were broken or what the security teams did to those men. My mind is going in a hundred different directions right now," I admit quietly.

He captures my lips with his own, crushing me to him, holding me and briefly letting me up for air... "Baby, I'm sorry if this puts stress on you. I was hoping to keep you sheltered from some of this, but unfortunately, that's not to be. I am not going to apologize, Katarina, nor would I do anything differently. Your security is not negotiable; I will take every precaution and do whatever is necessary to keep you safe," he says, his eyes holding mine hostage while his lips find mine, closing off any ability I have to argue. His tongue finds its way past my lips and into my mouth, exploring, and effectively imprisoning my tongue.

My body responds shamelessly, my hands running automatically through his hair, and around his ears. He scoops me up and within seconds, we're in the living area and then into the elevator and in our suite. He gently eases me out of his arms letting me down the length of his body so I can feel the significant hardness and arousal of his body.

"This sports bra leaves little to the imagination Katarina," he says, tracing the outline of my nipples through the material before pulling it over my head and discarding it. He rolls my nipples, squeezing them between his fingers before gently kissing and sucking one and then the other. His hands find my waistband, and he slides my shorts and panties past my hips letting them drop to the floor before leading me to the shower. He turns it on, guiding me under its warmth; leisurely soaping my body with the loofah... rubbing the slightly rough side across my nipples. "Hands over your head, Baby," he commands, using the tie of my bathrobe to secure them to the showerhead. "You trust me completely to tie you up; at the mercy of whatever I want to do to your body," he says, green eyes boring into mine intently. The abrasive material runs over my nipples again, making my insides ache. "I want you to trust me completely, Katarina, and I've decided to punish you every time you don't," he says. The warm water and his lips travel the same path, across my breasts and down to my navel. I know where his tongue is heading. He takes his time... nuzzling the soft hair between my legs, gently paving a way with his tongue, finding that special little place that drives me crazy. He slides my legs apart even wider, and I am completely exposed to him. I feel myself getting close, and his tongue moves to a different spot.

"Honey," I moan, "I'm right there..."

He pays no attention and continues his slow game of torture; his hands grasping my hips, firmly keeping me in one spot so I cannot move or find release. He continues; my hips and legs are reaching the breaking point from holding this position. "Are you going to trust me,

Katarina?" he asks, holding me with his eyes. He is completely in control.

"Yes, just please, Chase."

"Tell me what you need, Katarina?" he asks.

"Make me cum, Honey," I moan. The area between my legs is throbbing and frustrated at the loss of his tongue.

"All in good time, Baby," he says, spinning me around to face the wall. The robe sash quickly adjusts to accommodate the new position. He rubs my back and hips with the soapy loofah.

"Spread your legs wide, Katarina. I want you completely exposed to me when I spank you," he says huskily. He's actually going to spank me tied up in the shower... this is so hot. He continues soaping me and then his hand connects with my wet and soapy backside. He delivers five more, in the same place. It is intense, agonizingly fueling the now desperate need inside of me. He spins me around to face him; slowly and methodically trailing light kisses against my overly aroused skin, and traveling lower.

"Spread your legs wide, Katarina," he commands again.

I spread my legs wide, shamelessly, wanting his mouth there. His tongue caresses the soft folds around my clit, achingly avoiding her, and then with expert skill, gently, but firmly stroking her. His hands on my hips allow him total control, and he strokes me until I am writhing, crying out and trembling against him, but he does not let it end quickly, sucking my clit until I have no more to give. He finally releases my hips and kisses the length of my body before untying me.

"Turn around and put your hands on the wall, Baby. I want to cum deep inside of you."

I gasp as he slides deep inside my still overly stimulated body and I find myself climaxing around him at his persistent urging as he loses himself in me. He gently washes me, letting the warm water rain over me and then carries me to our bed curling in behind me. I snuggle back into him. "Chase, I do trust you. I just don't want you to keep things from me. But you can punish me like that anytime," I say sleepily.

"Sssh... sleep now," he croons.

I wake from my nap a short while later and find Chase working on the patio.

"I see you have decided to get out of bed for the day," he says, looking up from his Mac.

I smile, recalling the reason for my fatigue.

"Baby, when you blush like that I just want to take you right back to bed and that dress is not helping. It may be difficult for you to get any work done with my eyes constantly on your breasts," he says.

"You behave yourself. I need to get some work done if we want this project to come in on time," I retort good-naturedly, opening up my Mac and settling in next to him at the table. "The IT folks were able to extract last year's patient volumes, and I need to get the simulation prepared for the user group meeting. They are concerned about the time it will take the lab and out scheduling in the room. Right now, those services don't take up anytime in the exam room," I say.

"Right, we just make the elderly and sick go stand in another line. I'd gladly pay for more spaces so the patient could have all the services provided in the exam room," he says.

"I know you would, Chase. But we have new NPs and physicians being hired so we can build a very load leveled schedule. I don't believe we will require more exams. They will have three per provider at the time they work if we plan correctly."

"I'm looking forward to seeing the simulation and the design," he says earnestly.

SIX

The temperature and warm breeze couldn't be better for working outside and the afternoon is absorbed by our work demands. I'm putting the final touches on some of the data graphs when I'm alerted to another incoming email. I read the message and can't help but smile.

TO: <u>KMeilers@TorzialConsulting.org</u>
  From: <u>CHPrestian@PrestianCorp.org</u>

I COUNT twenty-four emails just that I have been copied on. Do you have to be the one to handle all of the logistics? Surely half of these Renee could assist with?
C. H. Prestian
Chief Executive Officer, Owner
Prestian Corporation

TO: <u>CHPrestian@PrestianCorp.org</u>
   From: <u>KMeilers@TorzialConsulting.org</u>

HAS anyone ever told you that you are bossy, overbearing and a serious control freak!???
   Kate Meilers
   Project Consultant
   Torzial Consulting Firm

TO: <u>KMeilers@TorzialConsulting.org</u>
   From: <u>CHPrestian@PrestianCorp.org</u>

RECENTLY IF I RECALL CORRECTLY!! Now, hurry up and finish!

C. **H. Prestian**
   Chief Executive Officer, Owner
   Prestian Corporation

I LOOK UP, and he's smiling at me with that wicked grin, green eyes alight at the game. "You are incorrigible," I state.

"You've been working all day," he says.

"Five hours... hardly a full day," I say.

"It's what you accomplish that should be the measure of one's work. You just put together an entire simulation. I would say it was a full day's work." he says.

"I'm almost done anyway," I exclaim.

"Good, we should see if your mother would like to visit before dinner. Why don't you find out if she is done working?" he says.

Message: Meet us in the kitchen for a glass of wine?

Reply: Sure, just finishing up with some final edits.

"MOM'S just closing up for the day, she'll meet us shortly," I relay.

"Like mother like daughter," he says amused. His phone rings, and he answers it scowling. "Chase here. How long ago?" he says after a brief pause. "I want to know who they're working for. Find out fast and get back to me. I'll give Sid a call and provide them with a four-hour deadline. Once that's in place, you'll need to have the team prepared for an extraction. The locals are going to blow when they learn we're pulling out and I don't want Sid and his team caught in the crossfire." He pauses, briefly listening. "Thanks, Jay," he says before ending the call.

"Katarina, do you really want to stay and listen to this?" He looks tired, but his eyes are hooded and controlled.

"Yes," I say, sensing the urgency of the situation, but not really knowing how bad things are.

"Sid, Chase here. We've had more issues locally. Give them a call and tell them I've issued an order to pull out altogether if negotiations are not reached in four hours. It ends now, Sid. Jay's got the team on standby to extract you and your team. I'll call you back with diversion details; in the meantime, make sure they know the deadline. You're welcome, Sid. Stay safe and keep me posted."

Holy shit, what triggered all this? One minute we're going to have a little wine and the next minute it sounds like he's ordering an invasion. "Chase, what the hell is going on?"

"Let's go downstairs. Your mom is going to need a couple drinks to digest this," he says, appearing agitated. "Your mom's office and her home were broken into. Jay had both staked out, and they were able to apprehend all five men. Do you want to know this?" he asks.

I nod, fully aware I'm not going to like what comes next. "I just gave the order to have Jay's teams find out from the men what they were looking for and who they work for," he says, watching me intently, his deep, steely eyes never wavering. *Holy shit, this is bad.*

"You think they are trying to get to me through my mom?" I ask as the reality sinks in.

"The best way to get to me is to get to you, Baby," he says, moving his chair around the table to take my hand. "Do you trust me, Katarina?

"I told you. I trust you with my life, but I would be lying if I told you I wasn't scared."

He takes my hand kissing it. "You have nothing to worry about, Katarina. These properties are locked down tight; the United Nations couldn't get through the teams Jay has in place. Let's go and find your mom. We should probably break the news to her before she hears it from the police and her coworkers," he says.

Mom has beaten us to the kitchen and is enjoying a glass of red wine at the dining room bar. I hug her close and wonder how she's going to take this.

"Karissa," Chase greets my mom. "I hope you had everything you needed to work today," he says politely.

She laughs. "More than everything I needed, Chase. I actually worked outside on the balcony. The weather was perfect, and the view was absolutely fantastic. Best day of work I've had in a long time," she says.

"We worked outdoors this afternoon ourselves," he says, pouring us both a glass of white wine.

"I was going to give you a tour, but we've had some recent developments we should discuss. I've had the main veranda set up for the evening, and we can have drinks and dinner there," he says, leading us through the house onto the patio.

It's more like an outdoor dining room. The floors are stone, and the pergola is wrapped in a combination of yellow and orange honeysuckle giving off the most beautiful citrusy fragrance. In the far corner is a grilling station made of the same stone as the floor. On the other side is a large iron table with a colored stone top. I'm sure ten people could fit around it comfortably. He leads us to a smaller more intimate looking table in the corner of the patio.

"Chase, it's beautiful. I've run through the other side of the orchards where the walking trails meet, but the view from this side of the house is incredible," I say, taking in the expanse of groves along the lake.

"One of my favorite places to relax, especially when the trees are in bloom," he says, pulling our chairs out for us. Two bottles of wine are chilling on the table, and Chase refills my mom's glass. I smile briefly, knowing he's trying to relax my mom before he tells her about the break-ins. A server places a large platter of bruschetta, sliced bread, oils, cheese, nuts, and olives on our table as Chase continues to make small talk with my mom. I have not met him and vaguely wonder how many people Chase employs to care for his home.

"Karissa, Katarina and I received some disturbing news today and thought we should bring you up to speed," he says, bringing me out of my reverie.

My mom sips her wine, eyeing Chase warily. "Karissa, we just learned that both your office and home have been broken into," he says.

She gasps, not expecting that for news. "What do they want, Chase?" she asks.

"They are trying to get to Katarina. They must know it is the best way they have of turning my position. They probably know of our relationship and think if they get to her I will negotiate. We have teams working to find out who the perpetrators are right now and will put plans in motion as soon as we find out. I would anticipate receiving a call within the hour. Additionally, we are working to quickly finalize negotiations overseas. We should learn in a few hours if they are going to accept our last offer. If they do not, we'll need to pull out... simple as that. I'm just glad you decided to come with us. While I have no doubt my teams would not have allowed harm to you, I feel much better with you under our roof," he says.

"I don't know whether to say 'thank you,' or be pissed as hell at you for getting my daughter in this situation," she says, eyeing Chase with a scowl.

"Mom, he was very honest with me early on, and I knew that being in a relationship with him meant security was going to be part of the package. I'm not particularly fond of it, but Chase is not going to let anything happen to us," I explain.

She takes a sip of her wine, contemplating everything she's heard. "Well, I guess there are worse places to be if you have to be under protection," she says lightly, swirling her wine as she finishes a piece of the bread. Dusk begins to settle and automatically all the trees in the corners of the patio are lit up with tiny white twinkling lights, turning the entire veranda into the most beautiful space.

"Karissa, did Katarina tell you that she saved a man's life while we were in Aruba?" he asks. I feel the warmth of my blush rise, as I am sure he realizes I did not, because it may have led me into a discussion about him with my mom.

She gasps. "No, she most certainly did not. What happened, Sweetie?"

"It was nothing, Mom. Really, anyone would have done the same thing," I say glaring at Chase, who is trying to cover his amusement at my outrage.

"The man would have died if it were not for your courageous daughter," he says barely containing his amusement as my mom continues to gush on about how proud she is of me. I scowl at his blatant attempt to divert attention from security issues to me.

"I hope you both like Italian," Chase intervenes, finally taking pity on me and distracting my mom from her fixed line of questioning as dinner is served.

"This is Gaby's chicken marsala. She makes it with a mustard mascarpone sauce that rivals any of the best Italian restaurants in Chicago," he says proudly.

"Chase, this is to die for," my mom murmurs appreciatively. I may need to find that pool tomorrow and wear off a little of our recent meals," she exclaims.

As the waiter clears the table, Chase seems distracted, looking down at his lap. I'm sure he's on his phone, and I feel a slight chill of apprehension at the thought of what may be transpiring. He glances up, catching me watching him. I look down in my lap and click on his message.

Message: Stop worrying!

Reply: Is everything ok?

Message: It's under control.

"I'm going to give you and Katarina some time to catch up. I need to take care of a few things. They'll be serving chocolate Italian cream cake soon. Have a glass of wine, and I should be back to catch a piece of cake shortly," he says, giving me a firm kiss. "Now stop worrying or I will begin to think you don't trust me and punish you again," he whispers so only I can hear.

I can't help wonder what he's up to as he leaves the veranda. He said he should know in about an hour what the guys that broke into Mom's place were up to and who they worked for. I shiver slightly at the implication, realizing I don't want to contemplate what may be occurring to get that information.

"Sweetie, did you hear me?" my mom asks.

"Sorry, Mom, I was thinking about something else."

"You are pretty serious about each other," she says.

"I'm in love with him, Mom. I just haven't told him, yet. Maybe it just seems too soon."

"Katie, you're living with the man. I think you are supposed to fall in love before you begin living together; at least, that's how it used to be. What the hell do I know? He's clearly in love. He never takes his eyes off of you," she says.

"I think he cares a great deal for me, but he's never told me he loves me," I say.

"Katie, are you blind? The man is absolutely head over heels. It worries me greatly that I find my daughter in the same quandary that I was in twenty-six years ago," she says.

"Oh, God Mom, with everything that happened, I never thought to call you and set things straight on that account. I am so sorry."

"Set me straight on what, Katie?"

"Mom, I was so caught up with everything going on that I didn't tell you. Chase is not involved in drug trafficking at all. We had a long conversation about it after I got home from the hospital. I just forgot to mention it to you."

"I see... and you believe him, Katie?" I can see the question clearly reflected in her bright eyes.

"Of course I do, Mom."

"I don't understand, what changed, Sweetie?"

"Nothing changed, I just never had the full story. Last year he was building a new factory in Saudi Arabia and was invited to close the deal on Prince Alfreita's ship in the Persian Gulf. Shortly after he left the boat, it was seized by Interpol, and they confiscated an enormous amount of cocaine in its hull. Interpol suspected Chase, due to his financial status and the fact that he was on the ship, but he was never officially charged."

"And because they didn't charge him you believe he's innocent?"

"Mom, he told me he didn't do it and I believe him. Unfortunately, it sounds like they are still watching him as though he were a suspect," I say.

"Baby, don't you think he may have told you that because he didn't want to worry you or for fear he may lose you if you knew the truth?" she probes.

"No, he's been pretty honest with me about things he's done that are not as orthodox as I would like and involved me in conversations he wouldn't have if that were the case," I say, hoping to alleviate her concerns and cease this line of questioning.

"And regardless of what he does you are in love with him and seem to have worked through your issues with that?" she asks.

I sigh. I know she only cares. I walk around the table and give her a hug from behind. "He means the world to me and I am so grateful you told me about you and Dad. I still have a lot of questions, but it helped me work through what I was feeling about Chase. Mom, he didn't tell me he wasn't a criminal until I had already decided to stay. He would have had nothing to lose by telling me the truth if that were the case. I think in his own way he really needed to know that no matter what, I wasn't going to leave. I can't imagine my life without him, so I'm glad that you made me look at it from that perspective."

"Okay, I just want you to be happy, Sweetie," she says.

"I know you do, Mom. I am still trying to absorb everything about my dad, though," I say.

She pats my hand. "I just hope one day you will be able to understand it all and forgive me," she says.

"Mom, there's nothing to forgive. I'd be lying if I told you I wasn't shocked, but there's no blame. You were young and look at me; I almost threw away what I have with Chase. I know this is probably your worst fear, but I can't stop thinking about meeting my dad," I say contemplatively.

Her eyes grow wide. "No, Sweetie. You don't understand. It's not like you are just going to waltz into his life and things will be okay. The immediate family and others that they work with will not allow it, and I am scared to death of what they may do when they find out about us," she says. I can see the deep-seated fear she has been hiding from me all these years, but I have to be honest with her.

"Mom, I'll be the first to say that I have no clue what you've had to deal with. I'm sure there is a reason for all of your fear, but it's all I've been thinking about," I say, immediately remorseful as I see the pain reflected in my mom's eyes, but at this point, unable to stop. "Mom, I have a father that doesn't even know I exist."

"Katie, don't you think I've thought about that for years? If I had believed for one moment that there was a way to safely go back I would have done that so you could have known your father. It's all I've thought of for years."

"I need to meet him, Mom. We'll find a way that is safe. Chase will help us," I add, trying my best to alleviate her anxiety.

"You have the same damn stubborn streak as your father," she says, clearly frustrated and still deeply disturbed at the prospect.

I sense his presence before he says a word. His eyes are raised in question at the quiet that has fallen over the table, as he settles into the seat next to me. The tension is palpable and uncomfortable between my mother and me. I know it is her fear, but I want to meet him. Chase begins telling us a story that was in one of the local gossip columns, as if nothing is amiss and we are soon laughing at his extraordinary tale of one of the wealthiest women in the country being arrested for indecent exposure.

Alone in our room, my curiosity can no longer be contained. "Chase, I'm dying to know what happened," I say half wanting to hear it and the other part of me apprehensive. *Do I really want to know?*

He is quiet and doesn't respond. Instead, I watch as a multitude of emotions plays over his features and register in his dark green eyes.

"Chase, I just want to know what's going on. Is that so wrong?" I ask gently.

He sits in the overstuffed reading chair to take his socks and shoes off, eyeing me warily. He sighs. "On the contrary, it's probably quite reasonable. Sid's been in contact, and they are still holding out. They have about an hour before we cut the deal and pull out. In the meantime, Jay's team was able to find out that the men who broke into your mom's house are working for one of the men we are negotiating with. One of the younger guys is his nephew. Plans are in place to get to his uncle within the hour. If he's the only hold out behind negotiations, we may have just moved into a better position," he explains, as if what he's describing is an everyday occurrence. He is watching me, intently, gauging my reaction.

"Get to him, Chase? What does that mean?"

"Katarina, there are some things better left unsaid."

I try to remain passive, not wanting him to see my internal quandary with his revelation. *I asked him to tell me. I wanted to know. He is not going to give me all the details. I don't understand how I feel about it.*

His eyes are intense, and it's clear the path has already been set.

"You're not going to tell me?

"Katarina, we've gone through this. I am going to do anything necessary to ensure your safety and that is not negotiable."

"I get that, but you won't even share it with me?"

"No, you won't like what needs to be done."

"How do you know? You haven't even told me what it is that you're doing, but already you make assumptions that I won't understand or that I will be upset about it. Why don't you just tell me what you're doing?" I ask, walking over to the other side of the room to stand in front of him.

"Baby," he says, pulling me onto his lap. "It's a world that you know nothing about, one that I want to protect you from. The people we're dealing with are ruthless, and I want to keep you sheltered from those things. Is that so wrong?"

"Perhaps not," I say, noticing the deepening shadows under his eyes. "How much sleep were you able to get last night?" I ask, winding my arms around his neck.

"Not much, Baby. I'll sleep better after tonight," he admits. His arms fold around me possessively, and he nuzzles my hair.

"What was going on between you and your mom?" he asks.

"I told her that I want to meet my dad," I say, this time watching his expression.

"Indeed... and when did you decide this?" he asks.

"I can't seem to think of anything else, Chase. I mean he's gone his entire life without knowing I exist. I am only twenty-six years old, and I see what a great relationship you have with your dad. I want a chance to get to know him, but I am scared that it may put Mom in jeopardy. You never told me how you figured out who my dad was."

"That wasn't hard. I knew it was Carlos as soon as you mentioned your father was head of the East Coast Crime Syndicate and that your mom had left him years ago. The Lussario name is synonymous with the Syndicate and everyone knows the story about your mom. I think that's when he started running things a little differently."

"It's more than a little intimidating. What's he like?"

"He's well respected in New York and a man of very few words. People know what he expects and he doesn't have to ask. Our fathers have been the best of friends since long before I was born. He's more like family to me."

"I wish my mom weren't so opposed to me meeting him."

"Give me and our teams time to develop a plan and put security precautions in place and then I will take you to meet your dad," he says, pushing the hair out of my face.

"Are you worried about her safety, too?"

"We need to find out if her concerns are valid, but Carlos is not about to let harm come to her and I'm sure as hell not leaving yours to chance, Baby."

I run my hands through his hair and down the side of his face. I can't believe how much this man has come to mean to me in such a short time. Even with all the baggage that comes with him, I love him. I kiss him softly on the lips and feel his immediate response.

"I love that you are taking care of my mom and me," I whisper. *Come on... tell him you love him. Maybe it's too soon, and he doesn't love me.*

"Baby, if you keep squirming on my lap and kissing me like that, this is only going to end one way," he whispers. I wiggle against him purposefully, kissing him even deeper this time, teasing, and feel his growing hardness in response. I feel his hands on the ties of my sundress, remembering the first time he pulled it down in Aruba, exposing my breasts to his eyes for the first time.

"Katarina, what are you thinking about?" he asks, and I know by the twinkle in his eye that he remembers. His hands intentionally hold the ties to my dress in my full view.

"I'm thinking about the first time you pulled my dress down. I'll never forget that, Chase. You made me feel things I had never felt before and I wanted you to take me so badly. Pull it down, Honey," I plea.

"You need only ask once, Baby," he says, scooping me up and taking me to bed.

We're still wrapped in each other's arms, spent from our love-making when the phone rings. "Chase, here," he says, answering it on the first ring.

"Good to hear, Jay. No, would agree. Send the diversion and get them the hell out of there while it's quiet. Sid can continue final nego-tiations from here. No, they stay under wraps until both teams are safely home. Thanks for everything and keep me posted," he says, disconnecting.

"The uncle turned, and as a result, negotiations were accepted which means the locals probably won't riot, but I'm not leaving anything to chance right now, given the situation. Jay will have our team go in after Sid. When they're home, we'll make sure the boys are returned safely," he says by way of explanation.

My face must reflect my surprise. "What... were you not going to pester me all night until I told you?" he asks, raising his eyebrows in a silent challenge.

"Well, maybe," I admit, trying to focus on the fact that he is returning the boys home safely and not everything else that has occurred over the last few days.

He pulls me into his arms and against his chest. His heartbeat is strong and steady, holding me captive in the sound of its beat. He gently pushes the hair out of my eyes and captures my lips with his. "I love the way you feel in my arms, Baby," he murmurs, caressing my hair. "What I didn't tell your mom when she asked how we met was that I was completely mesmerized. Your long auburn hair was hanging down in curls... most likely in your way, but God it was sexy. You looked up at me while you were checking his breathing, and your bright blue eyes were captivating. You were frightened but determined to keep him alive, and I couldn't help thinking what a lucky son of a bitch he was," he admits, rubbing the back of my neck with his hand. "Baby, from the time your eyes captured mine we were only going to end one way," he says, pulling me close. *Is that his way of saying he loves me?*

I swallow and try to calm my heart rate. "I need to share something with you. You're always telling me to trust you with my emotions and I am trying to get there."

"What is it, Baby?" he asks, his eyes gentle, showing their concern.

"Chase, I know you may not be ready for this, but..." I falter, nerves taking over and not sure now if this was such a good idea.

"Katarina, tell me what's the matter," he urges. *What if it's too soon and he doesn't feel the same way?* It's clearly too late. *No backing out now...* "Chase, I'm in love with you. I know it's probably way too soon. If you felt the same way, you would have told me, but..." *What the hell did I do? Why couldn't I just keep my mouth shut?* He pulls me close, squeezing me and kissing the top of my head before forcing me to look into his eyes, gently wiping a tear that has escaped down my cheek.

His eyes are warm, expressive green pools of desire. "Baby, is that seriously what you thought? Katarina, you've had my heart since Aruba, probably since the very first time I saw you. I didn't want to frighten or put any undue pressure on you. I'm sorry you've been concerned, but I wasn't willing to settle for less than you being able to trust me with your heart," he says, gently caressing my hair. *He loves me?* "I love you with all of my heart," he says, before capturing my lips with his own.

His phone interrupts our kiss, and he breaks off gently, tracing my lips with his fingers as he answers the call.

"Chase, here. He's only stirring up the locals to gain empathy for his cause. Of course, he's the only one with a point to prove. He'll get his nephew back when we get our team out. We are not negotiating damn it! Send the fucking message! He puts the phone down and pulls on his lounge pants. He is irate, and I've not seen him like this before. I can't help admiring the rippled muscles of his abdomen and chest as he paces, pulling a shirt over his head.

"I'm going to sit outside and have a drink; join me when you're done," he says, as I head to the bathroom to wash up. I slip a night-gown over my head, before going out to the heated balcony where he soon appears with a bottle of wine and two glasses. He takes the seat closest to me and pours a glass for each of us.

"So I take it they didn't get your team out, yet?" I ask.

"No, the diversion went as planned but at the same time upheaval in the locals started. The team had to make a decision to use force against the crowd or wait it out. They are hunkered down right now, and Sid's team is stuck until we negotiate our way out or take them out by force. They are working on the negotiation of his nephew for our team right now," he says, looking at me intently.

"Why are you staring at me like that?" I ask.

"Because I'm not sure how you feel about all this shit and I don't want to lose you. Your face is an open book, Katarina. You visibly blanched when I told you about the trade and it's clear by your expression just a few moments ago that it bothers you," he says earnestly.

"I am not sure right now how I feel, either, if I'm honest. I know I was pissed about all the security, at first, but I understand the situation a lot better now. I'm not sure how I feel about what some of the security teams have been asked to do, but I trust you're doing what's necessary to keep us safe. I may not like all of it, but I understand why you are doing it. I love that you are taking care of me, my mom and the rest of your family, Chase."

He looks visibly relieved. "Hopefully, we'll put this to rest shortly, and we can get back to normal. Come sit on my lap," he instructs reaching for my hand, pulling me into his lap and kissing my lips gently. "I want to hear you say you love me again, Baby," he coaxes.

"I love you, Honey," I whisper.

"Katarina, do you know what a happy man you've made me?" he asks, kissing me gently and pushing the hair out of my eyes. I kiss his lips and my fingers run through his hair and down to the nape, rubbing the back of his neck. "I love you so much. I don't want anything to come between us, Baby," he says, nuzzling my neck.

"I can't believe I was so scared to tell you," I admit.

"I'm sorry you were worried. I have to admit I was beginning to wonder if you were ever going to trust me with that information," he says.

"You knew?"

"Katarina, of course I did. You are not the type of person who sleeps with a man and moves into his home because you like him. You just needed time to work through your trust issues, Baby, but I have to admit it took much longer than I anticipated. In fact, I'm sure there's some just punishment for making me wait this long," he warns.

"You're so upfront and honest about everything else... I thought since you hadn't told me you probably just didn't feel the same way," I say.

"You needed to come to terms with your feelings without undue pressure. I did hold back intentionally," he admits, his dark green eyes glinting, eyeing me intently.

"I give up... you don't play fair," I pout.

He laughs, "Baby, I don't play fair... I play to win. I want all of you; mind, body, and heart and I admit holding out a little in the short term to get what I want." His phone rings, and he answers it immediately, "Chase, here. Good news, Jay! How long before they're in the air? Stall them if you have to, but make sure the team is home before you do. I know what they expect; stall them, I don't trust the bastards. Keep me apprised and text me when Sid lands. Thanks, Jay," he says, disconnecting.

"You're not going to trade?" I scowl more than a little surprised.

"Katarina, they had people in my father's building although they didn't get through the front door, your work, your mom's work, and her home. They have displayed a pretty fixed pattern, and I'm not about to take any chances with my team. I'm going to do what I feel is necessary until everyone is safe, Katarina. They will be returned when I know everyone is home," he says. The steely glint in his eyes is not to be argued with.

"I'm hungry, and this may last awhile. Let's go get a piece of pie and discuss just punishments," he says, changing the subject and grinning wickedly. "In fact, I've purchased a few more items that I think you may find quite appealing," he says.

I slip my robe on and follow him into the dining room, taking a seat at the breakfast bar while he pulls out an apple pie and another covered with whipped topping and chocolate shavings.

"Preference?" he asks grinning, and I know he's trying to lighten the mood. Hopefully, this will all be over soon.

"Of what, pie or paddles?"

"Curious?"

"Umm, yes. What did you buy?"

"Anticipation and patience, Katarina. All in good time," he says, eyes alight with amusement. "Apple or Chocolate Cream?"

"Can I have a small slice of both?" I ask, as they both look delicious.

"Great idea," he says, cutting each of us a not so small piece of each. His phone rings, and he picks it up. "Fuck," he exclaims, taking me by the hand and leaving me no choice but to follow in his wake.

"Do they have Gaby and Karissa? Ok, I'll let you know when we're on the interior radio. He disconnects, keeping me moving towards the elevator, but pushes something on the wall and a panel opens. He guides me into the elevator on the right. Two elevators.

Holy shit, just like the fucking espionage movies. Chase runs his finger over a keypad, and the elevator starts to move. "Katarina, we haven't walked through security procedures yet, but your fingerprints have already been assigned an authorization for the safe room," he says.

"In the event I wasn't here, you would just swipe your finger over the digital display. Jay has already given you full authorization. In the event you didn't have it, you could not get into the lower level or the safe room," he explains. The elevator comes to a halt, but the door does not open.

"Katarina, once the elevator is activated by an authorized finger-print, it will take you to the lower level, but will not open without visual recognition, which is why it's equipped with the digital surround displays," he explains. I shudder to think of the implications of that need.

"Let's move," he says, guiding me through the door as it slides open, down a hallway to another gate. He punches a set of numbers into the security system which sets off a voice recording that asks for the password. He leans into the speaker above the keypad and says, "Surprise" and the door in front of us opens. "We'll talk about it later," he says, seeing the question in my eyes.

We walk through an almost identical replica of the living room and dining room upstairs. The door slams closed behind us, and my mom crosses the room, and then hugs me tightly. "Katie, what the hell is going on?" she says, glaring up at Chase.

Jeez. What the hell is going on? I feel like we're in some psychobabble movie.

Gaby comes out of the kitchen and places two apple pies and two chocolate cream pies on the table in front of Dereck and Sheldon, who are engrossed in what appears to be a floor plan of sorts. I look into Chase's eyes, and immediately know the answer. Everything is planned down to the smallest detail. Of course, she would have enough food for all of us, prepared ahead of time, just in case.

Unfuckingbelievable! Dereck hands Chase what looks like a walkie-talkie, and he pushes a button. "Everything's set, Chase. Communications are clear, the teams are about to hit the air, and we'll make the exchange. We're monitoring the wave and will keep you posted if we hear anything else. Matt's teams are deployed to the airplanes sitting at O'Hare," Jay says on the other end. I glance up nervously and see the look.

Trust me, his eyes say. "Jay, he's just sending us a message... he wants his nephew home safely. Once our team lands make the exchange and connect me with him," Chase says.

"Will do," Jay says.

Chase turns to me and my mom. "Ladies, let's have a glass of wine, and I will fill you in on the details. He pours each of us a glass of white wine and my mother a glass of red.

"Karissa, I'm sorry things have escalated to this point. My teams are in good position and just about to take off stateside. However, the people we are negotiating with have deployed their own teams and are at O'Hare awaiting the exchange. We have security completely surrounding them, but in the event things heighten further it is better we are here. Karissa, there are clothes in the spare bedroom on this level that I hope you will find satisfactory along with toiletries, etc. He doesn't have to say a word to me. I know that I will find a large white robe in the bathroom, all my favorite brands along with a decent wardrobe of clothing hanging in the bedroom closet.

My mom contemplates what Chase has said, and nods her affirmation. "I'm a little shocked by all the security you have in place," she says, looking at me to determine my take. I shrug as if I'm completely used to it and try to suppress a smile as I see the twinkle of amusement in Chase's eyes.

"Karissa, our companies do a lot of good around the world, but there is the occasion that we need to deal with conflict," he says. The walkie-talkie looking device buzzes on the kitchen counter. Chase picks it up and pardons himself to answer it as he walks toward the kitchen.

"Katie, you don't appear the slightest bit bothered by all the security precautions or the danger," my mom admonishes.

"Mom, I trust him. He will keep us safe. If he had not insisted we go get you I cringe to think what could have happened to you," I reply.

"Need I remind you that if you were not involved with this man that we would not be in need of protection," she counters, and I wonder if she is reflecting back on her decisions about my dad.

"Mom, Chase is a good and decent man. He is trying to create more jobs for people that will benefit our country and theirs, but he wants to make sure the workers are treated well and I respect that. So many people have jobs because of the work he does. I trust him, and I love him, Mom."

"I'm just worried about your safety, that's all, Sweetie," she says.

"I know you are, Mom, but he and his team have protected me every step of the way. I wish you were more amenable to security."

"Katie, it's not that I don't appreciate the security team's efforts. I'm more concerned about why the need exists."

"I know, I feel the same way, but at the same time I support the work that Chase is doing and with that comes the shit we're experiencing right now. I wish it didn't, but it does."

We finish our wine and Mom catches me up on some of her work gossip. She's known for marketing some of the biggest names in show biz and helping them keep a quiet, low-key lifestyle when at home in Naples. She regales me with a story about one of her clients who just built a house on the coast with a twenty stall boat garage. Chase returns as she's telling me how outraged he was when people were snooping around his property and then how he hired a publicist to leak stories when he was no longer of interest.

"Ladies, the exchange has been made, and the planes are on their way out of O'Hare. We can go back upstairs and should be able to sleep in our own beds this evening," he says.

"Good, I have a little work to get done tonight," I say.

"Katarina, undoubtedly it can wait until tomorrow?" he asks.

"I have a few things that need to get done yet tonight," I counter, watching the expression on his face. After a day like today, I just want to bury myself in my work.

"The last few days have been fraught with negotiations, Katarina. One more would not be a problem. There is absolutely nothing that if not done tonight will have a severe impact tomorrow," he insists.

"You are absolutely infuriating sometimes," I retort, noticing my mother's failed attempt to conceal her smile. I scowl at her.

"What?" she asks in response to my glare. "It's nice to see that someone else besides me thinks you work too much," she states.

"Mom, you are supposed to be on my side," I exclaim.

"I am on your side. Maybe if you stop working so much, we'll be able to see each other more than once every few months," she says.

"Clearly I am not going to win with the two of you," I counter.

"I'm glad you realize the futility," Chase says, his tone quiet and uncompromising.

"It will wait until tomorrow, but we are so not done with this conversation," I retort, ignoring the set of his jaw. *He can be so controlling and so exasperating, sometimes!* I pass Derrick and Sheldon on the way to the kitchen and see Derrick's eyebrows rise having evidently overheard my outburst.

"Gaby, we got the all clear. We can go back upstairs now," I say.

"Great news! I was just going to make peach strata for breakfast, but I can do that later," she says.

"Let me help you get things upstairs. I'm sure that chocolate cream pie is not safe if we leave it for Chase to carry."

"Surely that young man would have it gone before we got halfway upstairs," she says laughing. We leave most of it until morning but take the pies and cheese upstairs.

"Should I cut a few more of the pies?" I ask, knowing that Chase and the others will soon be upstairs.

"Kate, you don't have to do that. I heard you mention you still have other work to finish," she says, seeming a little flustered.

I sigh. "Gaby, I do have a little to complete before tomorrow afternoon, but it's more a way to keep busy. And, he can be so bossy! You know, all the security, safe rooms; it's just a little much sometimes."

"It does take some getting used to and I have to admit he is a rather intense young man. I recall when Chase first hired me thinking Lord, what have I gotten myself into. I can't imagine wanting to be anywhere else now, though."

"That's how my mom described him when she first met him," I say, smiling at the memory. I can see how much you care about him and know the feeling is mutual," I say, uncovering the pies.

"You don't have to help," she says.

"Gaby, I love being in the kitchen. Besides, I know as soon as Chase has everything settled he is going to be ready for a huge slice of each of your pies. In fact, we were just raiding the kitchen when he got the call that we had to go downstairs," I admit.

"Heisters, I can't keep dessert in the house to save my life with the likes of you two around," she clucks. She pulls a couple knives out of the butcher block and hands me one.

"I suppose everyone may be a little hungry after a night like tonight. I'm going to put some decaf and regular coffee on to brew. I'm sure with everything going on that half of the boys are sure to be on duty tonight. Derrick and Sheldon will want pie, and I would imagine Jay and Matt won't be far behind." It does not take us long to get dessert ready and in short order, she pulls out the vanilla ice cream. "The boys will probably want a little ice cream, too." She clearly loves taking care of everyone, and I can see why Chase cares so much about her.

"Gaby, let me help you peel peaches for the strata. Chase is going to be a little bit, and I'd rather do this right now than the work I have upstairs," I admit.

We're laughing at one of Gaby's jokes and peeling peaches when Chase walks in. He grins widely at the site of the pie, ice cream and coffee we have laid out.

"I'll let the guys know you have food set up in the kitchen," Chase says, poking his head back through the door to alert the men.

"Where's Mom?" I ask.

"She retired for the evening. I think she's had enough excitement for one day," he says.

"She's not the only one," I say, reaching up to pull the ceramic bowls from the cabinet.

We dish up dessert for everyone and finish peeling while we listen to the guys talking about the day's events. I feel his eyes on me, and look up. His steely green eyes bore into me. *What are you staring at me like that for...*my eyes flash? He raises his eyebrows in response. He is so hard to read sometimes. It's almost two in the morning when everyone winds down and starts to leave. Chase shakes hands with each of the men, thanking them for all they did. He treats everyone that works for him with such respect. We're finally alone, and he pulls me into his arms, crushing me to him, capturing my lips with his... parting them to explore.

"Baby, he moans... I've wanted to kiss you in this kitchen all night."

"Something about kitchens that I should know about?" I tease.

He takes my hand and places it on his crotch, and I can feel his cock throbbing as I rub it over the constraints of his jeans. "Take your panties off and bend over the table, Baby. I want to fuck you from behind."

How can he make me moist, just by talking to me like this?

He lifts the bottom of my robe to watch. I slide the white lacy high cut panties down slowly past my hips and over my thighs, letting them drop to the floor and hear his breath catch.

"Now turn around slowly, and bend over the table, Baby," he urges, guiding me with his hand on the small of my back. "You have the most beautiful ass, Katarina," he says, caressing my skin and splaying his hands over my hips. "I want to cum deep inside of you while you shake on the end of my cock, Baby."

I'm bent over the kitchen table; half naked, completely exposed and soaked... he hasn't even touched me yet. I hear the zipper on his pants and feel his naked hardness press into me. "Spread your legs wider." As I do, he rubs the end of his cock between my legs, wiping my wetness from one end to the other over my clit. "Baby, you're always so wet for me. Is this what you're waiting for?" he asks, pushing his cock into me with one deep thrust.

"Oh, yes, Honey," I moan.

I try to push back, but he controls my movement with his hands on my hips. "Slow, Baby, feel me... inside of you, growing and throbbing. I'm going to drive you crazy now," he says, leisurely pulling out and then grinding right over the very spot that leaves me senseless. "Is that the right place, Baby?" he asks huskily.

"Yes," I moan. "Please don't stop, Honey," I say as he pushes in over and over. I lift up against him, but he has a tight hold of my hips and instead keeps us in perfect rhythm.

"Slow, Baby... I want you to cum with me tonight..." he says, pulling me into him as he thrusts, penetrating hard. I have lost all track of time as he drives me right to the edge, and then begins anew, over and over. "Now... Baby, cum for me," he finally urges, and I can no longer control myself as I shake around him, reveling in the feel of him releasing deep inside of me. He prolongs our pleasure, rocking us together, as we slowly come back to earth.

"Katarina, I think you were made special for me, Baby," he says in my ear, slowly easing out of me. I hear the zip of his pants, and as I start to stand up, he slides my panties in-between my legs, and scoops me into his arms, carrying me upstairs and into the shower. I'm suddenly exhausted from the emotion of all of the events this evening, and the shower feels warm and inviting on my tired body.

I move in closer to get under the water with him and his eyes lock with mine, that same look. "Chase, why are you staring at me like that? You had that same look in the kitchen earlier, too."

"Did I now?" he says, smiling mischievously.

"You know you did, now tell me," I say as he soaps the loofah up, slowly washing my neck, breasts, and belly.

"I could spend all night making love to you, Baby. I think, instead, though, I am going to get you washed up and tucked in for the evening. You're starting to get dark circles under your eyes and need a good night's sleep," he says.

"So, you're not going to tell me?" I ask.

"No, I don't think we'll have story time tonight," he says.

"Chase, you don't play fair. Seriously, how's a girl supposed to keep up?" I pout.

"Baby, I told you before, I don't play fair... I play to win. Now be a good girl and turn around so I can wash your back and that beautiful ass of yours. I finish drying off, and he holds my robe open for me, tying it loosely around me. Let's get you tucked in now," he says, guiding me to bed. He lies down beside me and curls me into his arms. The last thing I hear before I fall asleep is, "I love you, Baby."

SEVEN

I wake to an empty bed and realize it's almost nine a.m. Not so late, really, when you consider how late we were up, but I have tons to do. I get to the gym, and there are now two giant treadmills in front of the window and one has a large red bow around it with a card perched on the digital display.

Katarina,

For days weather or circumstances don't permit you an outdoor run. I hope you like it.

Yours,

Chase

IT LOOKS VERY similar to his, but apparently a newer model. It takes me a few moments to figure out the bells and whistles, but soon I've got my rhythm down and am listening to my favorite playlist. Just as my cool down song comes on my phone cuts in with a message. I look down and smile.

Message: Are you awake?

Reply: Working out on my new treadmill. Love it!

Message: Glad you like it. Come and eat!

Reply: Hope you left me some peach strata.

I WALK into the kitchen to hear Chase talking to Gaby about my question about the peach dessert. She looks up at me and laughs. "I'm glad we made two pans last night. The boys were in early for coffee, and they cleaned out one of them," she clucks, bringing me a plate. The cinnamon and nutmeg combined with the peaches smell incredible. I take a bite and murmur my appreciation. "Gaby, you are truly the best cook in the world. This is absolutely delicious," I praise.

"Well, you helped make it," she says.

I laugh. "I'm sure peeling some peaches doesn't account for how it turned out, but anytime you need a peeler to make a breakfast like this, I'm your gal!"

"Katarina, we're going to spend tonight here and then head to New York tomorrow. We'll be there until Thursday and then stay in the city when we return for a couple days. I sent Mary the plan for the next few days, and she will coordinate rescheduling any meetings for the two of us that can't be done remotely," Chase says.

"Okay," I say, finishing my strata.

"What, no arguments this morning?" he asks, his eyelids raised in question.

"No, I told you, I trust your judgment with security. In fact, I'm a little surprised we're leaving as quickly as we are," I admit.

"Glad to hear that. Yes, there has been a turn of events with negotiations and it's highly unlikely anyone would take a chance on destroying the position they are in," he explains.

"I think I'm going to work outside on the terrace then. I have a ton to get done since I didn't work last night, and it's a beautiful day," I say.

"Good idea, I'll join you later if I can," he says.

"What no argument this morning?" I ask, finishing my pastry.

"No, working outside during the day seems perfectly logical, while working past midnight on things that don't require your immediate attention does not."

"Of course, you would know about not working until all hours of the night? I think this may require further discussion later," I say sweetly, walking around the table to kiss him lightly on the lips, aware of the challenge in his eyes and Gaby's smile as I pass her on the way upstairs. I pull on a cami and yoga pants and open the french doors to the patio. A large carafe, along with creamer and cups has been laid out on the table. The light breeze from the lake has added a little briskness to the air. I step back into the bedroom to pull on a sweatshirt before pouring myself a hot cup of coffee and firing up the Mac.

TO: <u>KMeilers@TorzialConsulting.org</u>
   From <u>TParts@ Martel&Sons.org</u>
   CC: <u>CHPrestian@PrestianCorp.org</u>,
   <u>JWarling@TorzialConsulting.org</u>

AS REQUESTED, I have not spent much time creating different drawings with additional exam rooms, but I believe your idea of providing the physician group with a simulation is a good one. They still seem quite concerned about the number of rooms, and this may alleviate that. I would like to attend if scheduling allows and appreciate your offer.

THANKS,

TERRY

TERRY PARTES
   Lead Architect
   Martel and Sons

MOST OF THE emails are easy reads and simply informational. The land contract is going well, and there are no issues with the footprint even coming close to property lines. I was hoping to see the soil assessment completed by now, but no news is good news at this point. Jenny has sent me quite a few copies related to metrics on other recent projects, and I quickly respond to those. The last one makes me laugh.

TO: KMeilers@TorzialConsulting.org
    From: JWarling@TorzialConsulting.org
    CC: CHPrestian@PrestianCorp.org

DEAR KATE:

I have not seen you for ages! I believe you are working entirely too hard if you no longer have time to spend with your best friend. In fact, as your best friend and need I remind you, boss, I may feel it necessary to renegotiate your contract!!

JENNY

JENNY WARLING
CEO Torzial Consulting Firm

TO: JWarling@TorzialConsulting.org
    From: CHPrestian@PrestianCorp.org
    CC: KMeilers@TorzialConsulting.org

JENNY,

Katarina and I are planning to be back in the city Thursday. Are you available for a noon lunch at Prestian? I'd like nothing better than to discuss renegotiations of her contract.

THANKS,
  Chase

C. **H. Prestian**
  Chief Executive Officer, Owner
  Prestian Corporation

TO: <u>CHPrestian@PrestianCorp.org</u>
  From: <u>JWarling@TorzialConsulting.org</u>
  CC: <u>KMeilers@TorzialConsulting.org</u>

CHASE:

ACTUALLY, I am free and lunch sounds great.

JENNY
  Jenny Warling
  CEO Torzial Consulting Firm

HE AND I have discussed the Prestian facility projects at length, and I have conceded to work on Prestian Corp projects exclusively, but now what is he up to. And Jenny is in so much trouble. In fact, I reach for my phone and text her.
  Message: What the hell are you up to???

Reply: Just having a little fun. You deserved it! You haven't called me in days!

Message: We were a little busy!

Reply: I see...

Message: Not like that. Well, maybe! LOL

Reply: Well I'm glad he invited me! It will be good to see you!

Message: Agree... Miss you, too!! See you soon.

Curiosity gets the better of me, and I send Chase a text.

Message: What are you up to?!?

Reply: I see you have caught up to emails.

Message: You didn't answer my question...

Reply: No, I didn't.

Message: Well??!!??

Reply: Are you done, yet? You've been working for hours.

I look at the clock and realize it's almost three thirty in the afternoon. I don't know where the time has gone. It's been so relaxing working out in the fresh air. I feel a little fatigued having another restless night with the events of the last few days on my mind.

Message: Actually, I'm done for now. I'm going to take a baby nap.

Reply: Are you feeling okay?

Message: Yes, just a short night. I don't want to be tired too early this evening.

P.S.: I am still mad at you...

I LEAVE the french door to the balcony open and slip out of my sweatshirt and pants, tugging off my cami before sliding in between the sheets. A massive bang awakens me an hour or so later and I jump out of bed not knowing where it came from. Slowly, I realize it's the balcony door that has slammed shut from the breeze. The blue sky from earlier is now cloaked in an ominous grey and the whitecaps are crashing onto the shore. I close the door and am reaching for my bra as Chase walks into the bedroom. His eyes roam over my nakedness in clear appreciation. "Well, I just came to wake you up... I wasn't really expecting a show," he says, walking toward me and appraising the view.

"The breeze must have pulled the door shut with a bang, it woke me up," I explain.

He places his hands on my shoulders. "I love looking at your body, Katarina," he says, leaning down to kiss each of my nipples with his warm mouth making them instantly hard and erect. His hands slide down the length of my waist and rest at the top of the lace on my panties.

"Your body doesn't seem mad at me, Katarina. Whatever are you upset with me for this time?" he asks, eyes alight with amusement.

"You can't get me all hot and bothered and then ask me. That's not fair."

"I thought we had this conversation before, and you understood, I don't play fair. It's not likely to change, Baby," he says.

"Now tell me what I've done to deserve your ire," he says, stroking my nipples and then taking each into his mouth, tugging them gently with his teeth. He is slow and deliberate... licking each of them with his tongue, swirling them and gently sucking while I stand nude and exposed to him in the middle of our bedroom.

"Is that what you like?" he asks huskily.

"You know what that does to me," I moan as he starts his descent from my nipples, down my abdomen, exploring my belly button on his way south. His tongue stops at the lacy tops of my panties, and his fingers lift the sides as he takes the top of them between his teeth and pulls them past my hips, finding his way between my legs.

"Baby, move your legs apart and hold still, or I'll need to tie you up," he threatens, nuzzling the hair between my legs. "So soft and silky Baby," he murmurs, exploring with his nose. I am dripping wet in anticipation of his tongue. He urges me towards the bed and spreads my legs as I sink into its softness.

"Now, where was I," he asks, nuzzling between my legs, slowly exploring the folds with his tongue before allowing it to touch my clit. He is slow, insistent and holds me still as I writhe under him. He wraps my sex with the warmth of his mouth, and I can no longer contain the rush of my climax.

"Baby, I have to cum," I moan, and he brings me crashing around his face, sucking until he has taken every drop I have. He pushes my knees almost all the way back to my chest before he sinks into me. My body is so overstimulated I can only pant. "Slow, Baby," he says, pushing into me, and then pulling out, holding me on the brink again and again, until he finally brings wave after wave of desire crashing over me, allowing his own release deep inside of me. We lie together, spent and totally out of breath.

"Penny for your thoughts, Baby?" he says, looking into my eyes, and wiping the hair out of my face.

"I was thinking about how good sex is," I admit a little sheepishly. *Will he always be able to see what I'm thinking?*

"I'm glad you were pleased, Katarina," he says, his eyes sparkling with golden flecks. "I'm going to enjoy sharing new experiences with you, Baby," he says, getting up to start the whirlpool.

I check my phone to see if I've missed any messages. "I guess my mom is still working," I say.

"Your mom works entirely too much. She should slow down and experience life before she's too old to enjoy it anymore," he admonishes.

"Well, I'm glad to see that your aversion to working is not only directed at me. You really seem to have a thing for anyone working too much, which is odd because you work at all times of the day and night."

"I most certainly do and it would serve you well to remember that."

"Really, or what, some deliciously sexy punishment awaits me?" I ask, sticking the tip of my toe into the water. It is warm and inviting; I pour a little of the chamomile foaming bath crystals in before sliding into the whirlpool, laying back and losing myself to the relaxing feel of the surrounding jets bubbling around me.

"Careful, Baby. Your experience with punishment has been limited," he says, placing a glass of wine next to me on the granite ledge.

"Are you coming in?" I ask, recalling the emails he sent me when we first met almost ordering me to stop working so much. At the time, I thought he was an irrational control freak. I smile at the thought of his first emails. I had fair warning, that's for sure.

"What are you thinking about, Baby? You seem a million miles away," he says, sliding into the water across from me.

"Honestly, sometimes you look at me in a certain way, and I'm never really sure what to think when you watch me so intently. I'm curious what you're thinking. I've tried asking you, but you don't share. If I did that, you would end up torturing me with some divine sort of punishment," I exclaim.

"You are correct, Katarina," he states, his eyes capturing mine and holding them with his. I see that he's expertly averted talking about his feelings again. I take a sip of my wine and decide to change tact.

"Well, since I am in the sharing mood... I had a long conversation with my mom last night. I think we are both dealing with the after-shock of our conversation when I was in the hospital. She had no idea that I figured we were moving around because of her relationship with someone she worked with. It really surprised her. We talked about my dad for quite a while, and mom says his father passed away a couple of years ago, and he is the head of the family now," I say, trying to gauge his reaction, but his eyes are controlled and give little away about how he is feeling. "She still doesn't want me to meet him because she doesn't know what his family will do."

"I'm glad you told her about the pain of moving around and insecurities with people you work with, Katarina. You were clearly hurt as a young child seeing the grief your mother was in. I'm sure it must have been painful for her to be in love with someone and fear going back. She probably never realized you had absorbed any of this emotionally," he says.

"We've always been close, but you know deep down I think I blamed her relationship for my failed relationships with men. I don't really know how that makes any sense now, though," I admit, taking the last sip of wine.

"I was petrified when I found out that you owned Prestian. I've had such little trust in men at all and mainly avoided people I worked with. All I could think about was the devastation that it would cause my mom, and she doesn't even care that I work for you," I admit, still somewhat in awe of the situation.

"Well, technically you don't yet, but I'd like you to," he says.

"Chase, I'm extremely happy working for Torzial. Jenny is an amazing boss, and I owe the company a lot. She gave me a shot fresh out of school and exposed me to lots of different projects. I sort of work for you now and live with you. Isn't that enough?" I say, putting my arms around him, letting my hands explore the length of his torso.

His lips capture mine in a warm kiss while I continue my exploration of his chiseled body.

"We should probably go downstairs for dinner, or we are going to end up back in bed," he warns, stilling my wandering hands with his own.

"I'd rather stay here, drink more wine and go back to sleep." As if on cue the automatic water changer circulates, and the Jets send the warm water swirling around us.

"Baby, it's early, and you worked through lunch. Wine doesn't sit well on an empty stomach. Let's go visit with your mom for a little while, have a bite to eat and then we'll come back upstairs a bit later," he says.

"Nothing like being turned down flat," I state, pouting.

"Katarina, you have no idea what I'd like to do to you right now. However, I am bound and determined to teach you about the thrill of anticipation and delayed gratification. You see with prolonged anticipation the pleasure builds... so, while you're downstairs eating and having a glass of wine with your mom, I will be thinking of you with no panties on and what I'm going to do to you when I get you back upstairs. In fact, I believe we have some more training to do, don't we, Katarina?" he asks, watchful dark green eyes waiting for my response.

"Now think about what I'm going to do to you when we get back upstairs," he instructs.

I slowly rise out of the tub and step onto the stone floor, bending over to pick up my panties, slowly and purposely, so he has a nice view of my ass. I hear the intake of his breath as I bend almost completely in half and straighten.

"Katarina, you're playing with fire, Baby," he says, rising out of the whirlpool, and turning me to face him. "Turn around," he says, drying my wet skin with the towel from the warmer. "Close your eyes and trust me," he says, guiding me into the bedroom. "I was waiting for a perfect moment, but I can't think of a better time to give you this gift, then when you are completely nude and have completely and willingly exposed yourself to me," he says, as I feel the press and slight clicks of cool steel against my wrist. "Open your eyes, Baby."

I immediately focus on the slight weight of the four single bracelets that now adorn my left wrist. Each bangle is brilliantly polished, white gold in color and embedded with sparkling diamonds that adorn the top. I finger the little silver loops that hang from each and are encrusted with diamonds of their own. "Thank you, Chase, it's absolutely magnificent. I love it," I say, fingering the bracelets and the circular charms.

"You are welcome, now get dressed and I will meet you downstairs, before my resolve depletes and I take you right here," he says huskily.

I smile to myself as I rummage through the closet, determined to find something

hot, but not too over the top since we're eating in with my mother. I decide on a short fitted sweater dress with boots that reach just below my thigh allowing the edges of lace from my thigh highs to show. I find a pair of thongs slip them on under my dress and turn in the mirror admiring my new bracelet... game on! I stop in the bathroom to brush my teeth and hair, apply a small amount of makeup and lip gloss. There, ready... I am full of anticipation for the night ahead. Maybe he has something with this waiting game.

I take the stairs to the dining room, feeling somewhat flushed from the wine. Chase undresses me with his eyes... slowly, taking in every inch of me. I walk into the kitchen where Mom and Gaby are talking animatedly about a soup recipe. "Katie, you look fabulous tonight. I absolutely love the dress. Turn around and show me," she says. As I turn around for my mom to see the dress my phone swooshes. I look down and smile at the message.

Message: Now turn around and show me!

"Katie, it's gorgeous, the color is beautiful, and your bracelet is absolutely breathtaking."

"Thanks, Mom. Chase gave it to me as a gift," I say, before she turns her attention back to Gaby. I spot the remote on the couch in the adjoining room, walk over to it and bend over slowly, feeling his eyes on me.

Message: Good girl, Baby.

Mom pours me a glass of wine while dinner is being set and I meet Chase's eyes over the glass. "Katie, Chase and I were talking before you came down. It's a little tricky doing everything remotely. I want to go home and get back into my routine. Chase is going to have his security team fly me back and then stay on detail for a week or two. He'll bring you out soon for a long weekend and a tour of the bay," she says.

"Well, you two did have a nice little chat while I was changing," I say, as we take our seats at the table. "You think it's safe for mom to go back to Florida?" I ask.

"I'd prefer Karissa stay with us a little longer, but she's a grown woman and would like to return home. Jay will have a team with her," he says, as dinner is served.

"Well, it's certainly nice that some of us can be relied upon to make our own decisions," I say between bites, raising my eyebrows at Chase, who has his amused grin pasted on. I take another sip of wine.

Message: Pace yourself or it will be a short evening.

Reply: Bossy and Controlling!!!!!!!!!!!!!!!!!

Message: Anticipation and patience.

Reply: AND insufferable!

Message: Very nice dress, BTW. Looking forward to seeing it fall to the floor.

Reply: I forgive you. I'm anxious for training.

I TURN my attention to my mom who is in mid-sentence and regales us with her clients exploits as Gaby clears dinner. "Ladies, excuse me for a few moments," Chase says, following Gaby into the kitchen while we continue to visit. I listen to another story about her newest client and realize how much I am going to miss her when she leaves.

"Let's go find another glass of wine," I suggest, heading towards the kitchen. Chase is helping Gaby load the dishes into the washer when we walk in.

"The man has billions of dollars and helps with dishes. His mother sure did something right," my mom says aloud.

"Yes, it would appear she sent the rest of the crew home for the evening," Chase says.

"There wasn't much left to do," Gaby says.

"No, except clearing dinner, cleaning the dishes and the kitchen, on top of your own job," he says.

"You worry way too much, Chase. Now scoot before I decide not to serve dessert," she threatens, heading to the counter on the other side of the kitchen where she has a large silver and glass cake server sitting.

She places it on the breakfast bar before us, unveiling a carrot cake adorned with a cream cheese frosting. I almost laugh out loud as Chase takes a knife from the drawer and begins cutting into it while we talk. He begins to serve four dishes, but I put up my hand to decline.

"I'll have some a little later; I seriously need to let my food settle a little bit," I explain. Chase scoops some of the mounded frostings onto his spoon putting it to my lips. "At least, try this, Gaby makes the best cream cheese frosting in the world, and I do mean the world. I'll have you know I've stopped in many a bakery, and I have never found one as good, yet," he brags, winking at me.

"Eat your cake and stop that nonsense, now," Gaby scolds. I run my tongue over the frosting on my lips, licking slowly, enjoying the expression in his eyes.

"The wine and wonderful dinner have made me exhausted. I think I'm going to retire for the evening. I'll see you at breakfast before you head to the city," Mom says, hugging me tight.

"Gaby, I think Katarina and I are going to retire for the night, as well. The meal was excellent," Chase says as he guides me toward the elevator. He takes me into his arms as we enter the living area of our suite.

"You are driving me absolutely crazy tonight thinking about how bare you are underneath this," he says, spinning me around and slowly pulling the dress over my head, letting the material fall to the floor, leaving me once again bare and exposed before him in nothing but my new black lace thong. "So you are anxious for training?" he asks, grazing my taut nipple with his finger.

"You know I am," I say, running my hand along his shoulders and around his neck.

"Katarina, I don't want to go too fast with you, but you make it difficult to go slow," he says, kissing my lips lightly before taking my hands in his own.

"You're not going too fast. I love the way you make me feel."

"Then let's start with these," he says, fingering the silver rings around my wrist. "You see, they are very special bracelets, Katarina. Each bangle unlocks as I push them together, or can tighten around your wrist or ankle just as easily," he says, taking one of the bracelets and moving it to my right wrist. "See, they interlock, allowing me to restrain you at the pinch of my finger," he says, clicking the lock into place and effectively securing my wrists together in front of me.

"How does that make you feel, Katarina?" he asks.

"Excited and turned on," I say.

"Nervous or anxious?" he asks.

"Just excited," I say, riveted in place by the sheer carnal intent expressed in his eyes.

"You please me very much, Katarina. Such a beautiful body and so sensual," he says, trailing his finger down the length of my spine.

"I don't think you will need these tonight," he says, caressing the skin above the lace of my panties before pulling the scanty material over my hips and leaving them pooled around my ankles. "Let's place your hands behind you," he says, unlocking the bracelets and repositioning my arms behind my back.

"How do you feel now, Katarina?" he asks.

"A little more exposed actually, but very turned on."

"Yes, you are quite beautifully presented to me and indeed very vulnerable. Do you know what it means to me that you trust me so intimately," Chase says, gently rubbing his fingers over the curves of my breasts. "So lovely and erect," he says, tracing one nipple and then the other with the tip of his finger. There is a multitude of things that I would like to do to you, Katarina," he says, moving his hand from my breast to caress my navel while his other hand continues its scorching trail down my spine and along the curve of my ass. His finger travels along my lower belly, and I can feel my breathing begin to change as he caresses me. I inhale audibly as he moves below, fondling the softness of my mound with the cup of his hand, finding and lightly stroking my clit with his finger. "Baby, you are absolutely soaked," he says hoarsely, holding my ass firmly and inserting a finger deep inside of me, causing me to moan aloud.

"Katarina, I can't believe how sensual you are. I want to make up for all the sexual frustration you've ever felt, Baby," he says, trailing the warmth of his tongue up the length of my heated skin before kissing me and guiding me to bed.

"Having your hands behind your back is advantageous for lots of play, but this will work better tonight," he says, positioning me face down on the bed before removing the bracelets and repositioning my arms. "Let me know how this feels," he says, stretching them out in front of me, before locking the bracelets to the headboard."

"Better, not so restricting," I say.

He laughs. "Yes, while some nights I want you completely unable to move away from the sensations you're feeling, tonight however, the need to shift if something is uncomfortable is important," he says, kissing the tender skin of my ears and neck, and then trailing the length of my back with his fingers, before retracing the pattern with his tongue.

"Katarina, you have goosebumps," he says, running a finger over the delicate skin of my thigh.

"It feels so good, Honey," I say.

"I'll need to check that," he says, dipping a finger lower and inside of me. "So responsive, Baby," he says, rubbing the moistness, allowing his fingers to leisurely trail upward, circling the sensitive opening of my ass.

"Are you ready, Katarina?" he asks.

I nod my assent, and he pushes my ass cheeks apart slowly. "You're going to feel a lubricant now, Baby," he says, caressing my clit with his finger, while stroking the exposed view of my ass with a finger slick with an oily feeling substance. He traces its opening leisurely, flirtatiously taunting me before inserting it, allowing me to get used to the feel before introducing the second digit and gently stretching me. I unashamedly push back against him as I get used to the sensation.

"How does that feel, Katarina?" he asks.

"Full, good," I don't want you to stop," I say before something slightly rounded grazes against my skin.

"Baby, when I remove my fingers I'm going to replace them with something relatively no larger than my finger, just like last week. I will go very slowly, but you need to tell me if it's too much. It's important that you guide me, so I don't hurt you," he instructs.

"I'll tell you, Chase," I say. "You may feel a little pressure, and when you do breathe through it, don't push back until you're ready," he says.

I instinctively tense as I feel the round end of the object pushing against me. He pauses, slowly allowing me to fully acclimate to its feel before gently advancing it a small bit at a time. His finger continues stroking me and I moan softly, pushing back to take it in farther. "Don't stop... it feels so good," I say.

"Katarina, your thighs are shaking which tells me you are about to cum," he says, slowing and alternating the rhythm of his finger. I push back against him as he does.

"Still, Baby, let me guide it in and out of you, Baby."

"Stop, Honey, I can't take anymore," I moan as he explores deeper.

He pauses, slowing his rhythm in both areas. "Baby, tell me if you really want me to stop."

"God, please don't, I'm so close."

"I want to feel you cum for me, Baby," he says, resuming his rhythm and increasing his depth sliding its length inside of me, over and over as I build. I am helpless to the overpowering dam that breaks, leaving me trembling in its wake.

"That was so good," I moan incoherently.

"I was going to make you wait a little longer, but I know how much that frustrates you. We have all the time in the world for me to teach you about delayed gratification," he says, releasing my bracelets.

"Mmm," I murmur, stretching my arms and body.

"Baby, soon you'll be ready for me to bury my cock in your tight little ass, but not tonight. I want you to cum again, this time with me," he says, lifting my hips and impaling me with his rigid cock.

"Oh, God Chase. It's so deep this way," I say, pushing back against him.

"That's right, Baby. Push back and feel me deep inside of you," he instructs.

As I do, he takes me by the hips, pulling me toward him as he enters me, slow at first, all the way in and all the way out, teasing me. I push back against him impatient to have him deeper and am rewarded with a hard slap to the ass.

"Patience and anticipation, Baby," he says, guiding our rhythm, steadily increasing speed and depth. I feel myself building and tightening around him as he drives into me. My breathing is ragged as he gains momentum, repeatedly pushing against that special spot deep inside of me. All of a sudden the release is so near I can feel it.

"Honey," I moan.

He pulls me back, fast and intense against his chiseled frame, relentless, until I tremble around him and he climaxes with me, hard, shuddering deep inside of me. I collapse into the bed and he lies heavily on top of me, pushing my hair out of the way to kiss my neck.

"We're definitely going to have to do something about you holding still and telling me to

stop," he says.

I wake to the alarm on my phone and reach over to hit the snooze, trying to orient, groggy from the night before. I'm grateful for the Tylenol and water he gave me before I went to sleep or I'm sure I would feel much worse recalling Chase's warning about too many drinks on an empty stomach. As it is, my mouth feels like I swallowed cotton balls. I tap snooze on my phone thinking about last night, his mouth and tongue on me; how hot he made me before he flipped me over. The feel of the warm lubricant drizzling over my ass and the way he rubbed me before inserting his fingers into me. The progression from his fingers to the toy, stretching me while bringing me to orgasm. Remembering his promise, "Baby, soon you'll be ready for me to bury my cock in your tight little ass," before he made love to me. I am moist and aroused just thinking about last night. I get out of bed reluctantly and go in search of Chase.

Gaby has an excellent breakfast laid out of fruit, yogurt, and an egg bake. I take a seat at the breakfast bar and pour a cup of coffee, listening to Mom and Chase talk. I serve myself a generous helping of fruit and yogurt and Gaby smiles as she pulls an egg dish out of the microwave.

"I tried a little recipe with Egg Beaters for you. Your mom told me eggs aren't your favorite," she says.

"Gaby, that was so sweet of you. I hate that you went to the extra trouble, but thank you. This is absolutely delicious," I say, taking a small serving of the dish and trying a bite.

Chase sits beside me and puts his arm around my shoulders. "How are you feeling, Baby?" he whispers so only I can hear him. "A little tired and glad I took the Tylenol," I admit.

"Good. Jay's working to get the helicopter set. It should be ready shortly. Do you have everything you need already packed?" he asks.

"Almost, I just have to grab my laptop and makeup. Otherwise, I'm all set. I should purchase more makeup to keep in my travel bag," I say.

"We can have someone pick that up for you," he says.

"Actually, I was thinking of asking Jenny to go shopping, and I may even get a makeover. You know, a little haircut, new makeup," I say, as I finish my breakfast.

"There's nothing to makeover, Baby; you're absolutely perfect," he says, his dark eyes holding mine.

"I'll talk to her about it a little later. She loves to shop, and I do need a few skirts and a pair of boots," I say.

"I think you might want to add some lingerie to that list, too," he says so only I can hear.

"Chase, what time will Dereck and Sheldon arrive?" my mom asks.

"They're bringing the limo around to transport you to the airport now. Katarina and I will take the helicopter into the city once you leave," he says.

"He's only got one helicopter, Mom," I say, smirking at Chase. His eyebrows rise as he tries to hide his amusement.

"Karissa, the jet will take you back to Naples, Dereck and Sheldon will be traveling with you. You need to make sure you apprise them of your plans each night for the next day or so and don't deviate from that unless you alert them," he instructs.

"I will. Jay went through security with me this morning before you came down," she responds.

"Good. I'm going to get ready and let you and Katarina have a few moments," he says, leaving Mom and me to say our goodbyes. I give her a long hug, and she squeezes me tight. I am really going to miss her.

"We'll come to Naples as soon as we can and then you should plan to come here to visit again," I invite.

Chase walks back into the room and has changed into his executive attire. God, he looks hot. His suit has clearly been custom tailored for him. It follows the lines of his shoulders and hangs perfectly on the rest of his well-sculptured body. He captures my eyes with his own as they take in his body, and I see the small quirk of his mouth. "Are you ready Katarina, or do you need a few moments?" he asks, clearly amused.

I feel myself blush under his scrutiny. "I'll just grab a few things and be ready."

The morning flight to the airport is absolutely breathtaking with tree tops boasting their fall colors of orange, yellow and crimson show-cased with the dark blue backdrop of Lake Michigan below. The stark white Prestian corporate jet is awaiting us, and the flight crew welcomes us aboard. Matt and Jay head towards the security quarters located behind the cockpit and Chase guides me towards the middle of the plane and into the plush living space of the Gulfstream. We slip into the reclining leather chairs across from a small grey swirled marble table that is situated next to the oval window.

The jet is soon airborne, and the hostess places a carafe of coffee on the table along with cheese, nuts and fruit. Chase pours each of us a cup of coffee and nods towards the platter. "Are you hungry? You barely touched breakfast this morning," he says.

"I know. I probably should have taken your advice and eaten some-thing before I had the wine yesterday."

"Indeed. In fact, I don't think we discussed the consequences of your infractions yesterday," Chase says, tracing the circles of my bracelet.

"I didn't realize that it might lead to some deliciously wicked punishment," I whisper, glancing around the room.

"The door to the living space is closed, Katarina. Matt and Jay can't hear what we're saying, but they can see into the room unless I turn the camera off," he says, pointing to the app on his phone.

"So at a click of a button you are in total control," I say.

"You sound surprised. Does it bother you?" Chase asks, eyes raised mischievously.

"Your need for control?"

"Yes."

"Not usually."

"And at times it does?" he prompts.

"Only when you try to interfere with my work or when, you know..." I say, trailing off.

"You are blushing," he says, grinning.

"You are incorrigible!"

"I am, and speaking of which, we were talking about your infractions were we not?"

"So what else can you do with that little app of yours?" I ask.

"Come on, I think we've talked enough," he says, guiding me into the master bedroom and closing the door behind him. "You see for one, I can push this button," he says, as all the blinds over the oval shaped windows come down. He holds out his phone and selects a different button on the app and the fireplace ignites, he pushes another, and the lights dim. Now I want nothing more than to feel your naked body pressed against me while I make love to you," he says, kissing me.

Chase and Jay are already conferring about something when I come out of the bedroom and slip into the seat across from Chase. The captain announces the descent and the pilot soon connects smoothly with the runway. The limousine driver takes us through the city, quickly navigating morning traffic and pulls alongside an extensive chrome and glass sky-rise with the Prestian Corporation logo emblazoned on the side.

Chase grasps my hand and guides me to the elevators using a fob to enter the upper level. He stops to converse and introduces me to a few people as we make our way to his dad's office. Don is seated behind a great desk with a window behind him that overlooks the towering sky-rises and city beyond. "Nice to see you again, Kate," he says, standing to shake my hand and give Chase a hug.

"Good to see you, son," he says, waving us into the leather chairs across from his desk as he closes his office door.

"Kate, Chase told me about your situation. He may have explained that Carlos is a good friend of mine; our families go back some time. I don't know if your mom will remember me, but I was at their wedding. In fact, I couldn't quite put my finger on it when we met in Chicago, but there was something about you that seemed familiar. You look a lot your mother did years ago. Carlos was devastated when she disappeared and turned New York City and half the country upside down trying to find her. Chase asked me if I would talk to him and smooth the way for a meeting between the two of you," he said.

I glance at Chase, and he is watching my reaction. "I didn't realize that Don, but I knew Chase was working on a plan so that I could meet him," I explain.

"Kate, I'm not a man that beats around the bush. I've already spoken with Carlos, and I'd be lying if I said he wasn't in a little bit of shock about the entire situation, but he wants to meet you. Chase was adamant about having the utmost security, so if you are agreeable, he can come to our home tonight. I sincerely do not believe you will need protection from Carlos. He would never do anything to disrespect my home or family. Chase has already filled me in on the fact that his family and colleagues may not feel any warmth toward Karissa, but I can assure you in my conversations with Carlos that he feels nothing but remorse for your mom's fear and the situation you both find yourself in now. I do need to warn you, though, Kate. He is going to want to know how to reach your mother. I have told him that I am going to leave that up to you."

"I plan to be present for those conversations, Dad. No one knows where Karissa is until we have a plan with Carlos to ensure her safety," Chase says.

"Kate, do you want me to have your father come for dinner tonight?" Don asks.

"Yes, please. I can't thank you enough for talking with him, Don. I hope it was not a strain on your friendship."

"You're more than welcome, Kate. I think Carlos is in a little state of shock, but nothing could have made him happier than to hear that the woman he spent half his life in love with is not dead and that he has a daughter who wishes to meet him. I'll make the call and invite him to dinner," he says.

"Thanks, Dad. Katarina and I are going to work in my office for a while. Then I need to meet with Brian to go over some of the contracts for the medical facility expansions. I thought we could do that in person while I'm here," he says.

He guides me down the hall past Brian's office that has Brian Carrington, COO inscribed on the nameplate outside of his door and into his own. The room is as large as the one he has in Chicago with a view overlooking the city.

"Have a seat," he says, closing the door and sliding behind the large oak desk.

"Are you nervous?" he asks.

"I am, but I can't help be a little sad, too. All this time, he thought my mom was dead, and he didn't even know he had a daughter," I say.

Chase nods. "I am sure it was quite a jolt. That's why I asked my dad to talk to him. I wanted the news to come from someone he trusted, and that knew how much he cared about Karissa. We need to be prepared to answer his questions about your mom. He has spent the last twenty-six years loving a woman he thought was dead. He is going to want to find her. If I were him, I wouldn't be able to stop searching until I did," he says.

"I know, but it's just not my decision to make. My mom has to agree to meet him if that's what she wants, but she is terrified that members of the syndicate will try to hurt us if they learn about our existence. I don't get it. What could my mom possibly know that would make them feel as though she was a threat?"

"I think you can only be honest with Carlos and tell him exactly what you've shared with me, Baby. If he wants to meet her and she agrees, then he'll need to help us develop a plan to keep you both safe," he says.

He stands up. "Brian, come in," he says. I look up to see a tall man with shock black hair, bright blue eyes and a friendly smile in the doorway. "Good to see you," Chase says, shaking his hand. "You remember Kate," he says.

"Nice to see you in person again, Kate. Until you started working on the medical center project, I only had one person to deal with sending me email messages at all hours of the night. From the looks of my inbox, I now have two of you to deal with. Chase, I think you've finally met your match," he says.

"Indeed," Chase says, eyebrows upturned, watching me intently.

"Pull up a seat, Brian. I thought we could go over some of the contracts for the expansion since we're here, and I believe it would be helpful for Katarina to be part of the discussions," he says. The afternoon goes fast, but on the way back to his dad's house my nerves begin to get the better of me.

"Chase, what if Mom is right and I lead people right to her?" I ask, leaning into the crook of his arm in the backseat of the limo.

"Katarina, I think you need to meet him and hear what he has to say. It's been years, and things can change a lot with time," he says, pulling me close.

EIGHT

The Prestian senior home is every bit as impressive as Chase's with a long wooded drive into a private and secluded area outside of the city. The driver slows and talks with the man at the gate for a few minutes before the wrought iron gates lift allowing us entry into the estate just like at Chase's. The home is a two story colonial style with large white pillars and looks inviting. He drives around the large semi-circular drive and stops outside the front door for us. Chase guides me to the door, enters a code into the keypad and guides me into a large foyer.

"Chase... welcome home. I thought I heard someone," says a well-dressed petite woman with short blond hair who appears to be in her middle fifties. He gives her a hug and introduces the two of us.

"Emily, this is my girlfriend Kate, and this is Emily," he says, turning to me.

"Nice to meet you," she says to me. "Chase dear, make yourself at home. I was on my way out. You remember my granddaughter, Patrice?" she says.

"Of course," Chase says.

"Well, she plays flute and has a recital tonight. I'm traveling into the city to hear her play and plan to stay the night with my daughter and son-in-law," she says.

"Enjoy your evening, Emily. Next time we'll provide you with a little more notice and we can have dinner. Where's dad?" he asks.

"He got home about an hour ago and is still on the treadmill. I would imagine that he won't be much longer. In the meantime, make yourselves at home." she says, kissing him on the cheek as she heads outside towards the awaiting car.

Chase leads me up the winding staircase to a second-floor suite. The sitting room is furnished with a leather sectional, and a large screen monitor and Mac sit on the desk in the corner. The views from the expanse of windows are green treetops of pines and hardwoods as far as you can see, seemingly surrounding the entire property. The bedroom is furnished with a four-poster mahogany bed, another desk, and walk-in closet. The adjacent bathroom overlooks the opposite direction and is encompassed with a forest of green pine trees creating its own level of natural privacy. I open the door to the balcony, and go outside onto the patio, enjoying the cool crisp breeze from the beautiful autumn day. "You like it, Baby?" Chase asks, putting an arm around me from behind.

"I love it. It's so peaceful," I say.

"You have a lot on your mind," he says.

"Yes, I didn't think I would be quite this nervous."

"Let's go inside," he says, guiding me back indoors. I slip my shoes off and curl into the corner of the leather sofa. Chase takes his suit coat off placing it on the back of one of the dining room chairs, loosens his tie and takes off his shoes. He sits on the couch next to me and pulls me into his lap. "Baby, it's going to be okay," he says.

"I'm trying to think of what to say to him when I meet him. It's sure to be awkward... you know, my mom is going to be pissed, and I can deal with that, but the look on her face when I told her I wanted to meet my dad. I've never seen it before, Chase. She was terrified."

He pushes the hair out of my face and kisses my lips tenderly. Dad and I will be with you. It will be okay. Now rest your eyes for a little bit," he says, rubbing the back of my neck with his thumb and forefinger. I close my eyes and surrender myself to the feel of his hands massaging my neck and feel my body slowly begin to unwind and relax.

I open my eyes and realize I've been sleeping and am stretched out on the couch with my head in his lap.

"Feel better?" he asks, looking down at me and pushing a stray hair out of my face.

I nod, feeling his hardness beneath my cheek. I shift slightly, nuzzling him with my lips and breathing him in.

"Baby, if you keep that up there's only one way this will end. Let's save your energy to meet your dad. Why don't you get showered up first? I didn't want to wake you, but I have a little work that I need to complete, and your dad should be here within the hour," he says.

I take my belongings and head to the bathroom trying not to let my nerves get the best of me. I can't believe I am really going to meet my father. I have half a mind to call my mom, but I don't want her to try to talk me out of it or worry her needlessly. I peel out of my clothes and step into the warmth of the shower, relishing in the massaging sprays, taking the time to wash and pamper my hair, before drying off with the oversized velour feeling towel. I slip into a mid-thigh skirt, long sleeve belted blouse, and brown boots that only show a hint of my lace trimmed socks. I scrunch my hair, drying it slightly, but allowing it to hang in its naturally curly state, then add some hoop earrings and a little makeup, before I head into the living area.

Chase is already out of the shower and has dressed casually, in dress pants and sports shirt. He leads me downstairs to chat with his dad and have a glass of wine before the bell announces my father's arrival. The housekeeper announces Mr. Larussio, and a tall man just over six foot tall, with an athletic build, dark brown hair and eyes, walks through the door. He appears much younger than his forty-nine years, although deep brown sharp eyes and a smattering of grey flecks gives a hint to his real age. He stands erect, surveying the dining room and his eyes connect with mine as he walks into the room and shakes hands with Don and Chase.

"Don, thanks for inviting me. Chase, it's good to see you again," he says, his eyes never leaving my face. "You must be Kate," he says, extending his hand to mine. "You look so much like your mother," he says, taking my hand and brushing it with his thumb. I've been trying to picture what you would look like since Don told me about you. You're absolutely stunning," he says, and I try to conceal my blush.

Don hands Carlos a glass of wine and urges us to take a seat. Chase sits on the love seat with me, and Carlos sits across from us in a wing-back chair while Don makes himself comfortable on the couch adjacent to ours.

"Don tells me that your mother just recently told you that we were married and that she left. I wish to God that we could somehow turn back the clock and that your mom had not felt the need to move, but I don't blame her. I wasn't truthful with Karissa, and it must have been a shock for her to learn she had married someone other than a fine upstanding businessman. You can't know how thrilled I am that she is alive and have my assurance that there is no ill will towards her, only regret. I did not know that I had a daughter, Kate, but I am delighted," he says.

I feel myself relaxing at his words and Chase's hand on the back of my neck. "Carlos, I don't know if Dad shared everything with you or not," Chase says.

"I'm in love with your daughter, and want to make damn sure that her meeting you does not result in backlash for her mom or her. I assured Karissa that if her daughter wanted to meet you that they would be safe. I just need to make sure we understand each other upfront," he says.

"I appreciate your candor, Chase. I think a great deal of you and your family and couldn't be happier that you and Kate are together. We will need to develop a plan to ensure that if and when we acknowledge this publicly that my family is supportive or that we have counter measures in place to mitigate any risk to my wife or daughter," he says.

I look up at his reference to his wife, and he sees my contemplation. "Kate, I fell in love with your mother over twenty-six years ago. There has never been anyone but her for me. She is not dead and still legally my wife. You must know that I want to find her and talk to her, but I won't push you for information about her location."

Dinner is served, and the conversation is comfortable and relaxed. Don and Chase converse about the medical facility expansion, and I share some of the model's early successes before Don and Chase talk about its national development capabilities with Carlos. The evening goes by much too fast, and Carlos takes my face in his hands and places a kiss on both of my cheeks. "I can't tell you how pleased I am that you wanted to get to know me. You've made me a happy man tonight, Katarina. Please talk to your mom and if she wishes to meet with me, I am glad to do so, discreetly, with you and Chase present. You have my word that I will do everything in my power to keep you both safe," he says.

He leaves, and Chase pulls me close to his side holding me around the waist. "Are you okay, Baby?" he asks. His dad pours us a drink and waves us to take a seat.

"I'm fine, just a little overwhelmed with emotion right now. He seemed happy to meet me and obviously still just as much in love with my mom as she is with him. I didn't tell you this Chase, but in the hospital, my mom said that she still loves him. She was just too scared of what his family or the syndicate may do to us if she went back to Carlos," I explain.

"His brothers came into manhood after your grandfather passed on. There was a period I thought they would never settle down, but time changes everything," Don says.

"Thanks again for introducing us and allowing us to meet in your home," I say.

"You are more than welcome, young lady. I hope to see more of you and Chase now that this thing in the Middle East has blown over. I'm sorry you couldn't spend more time with Emily this trip, but we'll plan ahead next time," he says before retiring for the evening.

"Your dad is great," I say to Chase when we're back in our room and curled up in bed. "I was hoping my dad would be something like him."

"Were you disappointed?" he asks, holding me close.

"Not at all. He seems sort of old worldly, like your dad in some ways. I just can't put my finger on it."

"They grew up in hard times, Katarina, but with a high code of ethics where family is concerned. Are you going to tell your mom that you met him?"

"I am. I'm sure to catch her wrath at first, but she's still in love with him. I just don't think she ever thought there was a way around dealing with the family or syndicate. Maybe it will be different now that he is head of the household? Do you believe there is a way to keep her protected, Chase?" I ask.

"It's a grave concern, Baby. I don't know how to answer it just yet. If Carlos wants you and your mom in his life he will help me make it happen, but we're going to have to have a lot more conversation around this before I feel comfortable. We'll figure it out, but for now, you should get some sleep. We need to be at the airport early for a meeting back in Chicago," he says, curling me up in his strong arms.

We get off the plane, and I can't help but feel a little anxious as we arrive at the office and prepare for the user group meetings that Renee has scheduled. Once we have this information I'll be able to complete the simulations for the team and hopefully, alleviate the angst from the physician groups that will be practicing in the space. The helicopter ride is swift and as we land Chase helps me down and onto the helipad, guiding me into the now familiar tower entrance. Jay leads up the rear, and as we enter the building I'm surprised to see Matt here since he didn't travel back with us, but as he gives the all clear sign, I realize precautions are still being taken, and he's had his crew sweep the facility. I'm not sure if I will ever get completely used to it, but have to admit after the last week I'm glad they are with us.

"I have an all-morning meeting, Baby, but I've asked Mary to have lunch set up in your conference room. Jenny should be here around noon, and I'll join you a few moments after that," he says.

"I almost forgot that we were meeting her for lunch today," I say, kissing him goodbye.

As I walk into my office, I catch sight of a stunningly large burgundy vase sitting in the corner of my desk. It is filled with dozens of white long-stemmed calla lilies nestled in green foliage. It takes me back to the day I walked into my resort room in Aruba. There was a bouquet of white calla lilies in my suite that day, too, although nothing as elaborate as this one. There is a card with my name on it nestled among the flowers, and I gingerly take it out to read.

I open the card and in impeccable handwriting it says:

Katarina...

I am going to miss having you all to myself. Join me on a trip to where our journey began. I have made arrangements for a long weekend to Aruba at the end of the month.

Love,

Chase

Message: The flowers are incredible. YES!!!!!!!!!

Reply: Glad you like them.

Message: I love them! Calla Lilies always remind me of you and Aruba!

Reply: Likewise, Baby.

I smile to myself. I should leave him alone since he's probably in the middle of his meeting and I have so much to do. I open up the desktop and groan at the number of emails related to the exam room. I quickly sort them by subject to read the entire chain, frowning. We really need this simulation fast; it seems to be causing a lot of unnecessary angst for everyone. I flip over to Renee's incoming messages and smile. She really is very efficient, and I can't help but appreciate her outgoing nature.

TO: <u>KMeilers@TorzialConsulting.org</u>
   From: <u>RCampbell@PrestianCorp.org</u>

KATE:

You will see a succession of meeting planners on your calendar for pre-work and the actual simulation demo. I have scheduled a brief conference call with you and IT. Tim has a few more questions related to the data extraction that I was unable to answer. I have then scheduled time for you to review each of the three architectural designs that Terry's team has created. If I understood you correctly, we would use each model in the simulation to vet out any inefficiency at the same time.

Lastly, Mr. Prestian has asked that I put out of office holds on your calendar for the last Wednesday of this month starting at 3 p.m.

through the following Monday. I have taken the liberty of rescheduling appointments during that time as he notes you will be out of the office.

P.S. If you give me administrative rights I can not only schedule these meetings but send them on behalf of you right from your calendar, as well as accept them, too. This would significantly cut down on a lot of your email, and I am happy to assist.

Thanks,

Renee

Renee Campbell

Administrative Assistant

Prestian Corp Medical Center Project

TO: RCampbell@PrestianCorp.org
    From: KMeilers@TorzialConsulting.org

RENEE,

Thanks so much! Excellent idea! Done...

Thanks,

Kate

Kate Meilers

Project Consultant

Torzial Consulting Firm

I PULL two cups out of the cupboard above the granite bar as Renee walks in. "Would you like a fresh cup of coffee?" I ask.

"Sure, I was just finishing this, anyway," she says, referencing her cup and picking a decaf hazelnut. "My boyfriend, Corey, had the alarm set for three-thirty this morning. He and his crew had to leave early for a construction job in lower Illinois. They're building a new school and will be working long hours until they get the facility framed and wrapped for the winter. I couldn't get back to sleep after he left, so I have had more than enough caffeine for one day," she explains putting her selection into the machine to brew.

"The Keurig machine and coffee assortments were a gift from Chase when I first moved in," I say, nodding towards the large bronze sculpted holder. "Please feel free to use the coffee pods and brewer in here. Honestly, there's more here than I could ever drink alone. I think between the ones in the display and those here in the top drawer there are enough pods to last the two of us the entire year if not more," I exclaim.

"That's really sweet of you, Kate. The coffee is excellent. I finished sending out the documentation and everything is scheduled for the simulation. You have several standing meetings on your calendar at Torzial. You'll want to let me know which ones are critical that you attend or if you expect me to add an online option to them," she says.

We chat for a while, and when she leaves, I review preliminary information about the ground soil tests which had to be completed due to the intercity location and all the factories surrounding it. The initial test results look promising and appear that state approval should not be a problem.

TO: KMeilers@TorzialConsulting.org
  From: CHPrestian@PrestianCorp.org

GLAD TO SEE the ground looks good thus far.

C. **H. Prestian**
  Chief Executive Officer, Owner
  Prestian Corporation

TO: CHPrestian@PrestianCorp.org

From: <u>KMeilers@TorzialConsulting.org</u>

I WAS JUST READING THAT. What are you doing on email? Are you still in your meeting?

KATE

KATE MEILERS
   Project Consultant
   Torzial Consulting Firm

TO: <u>KMeilers@TorzialConsulting.org</u>
   From: <u>CHPrestian@PrestianCorp.org</u>

SHORT BREAK... Reconvening.

C. **H. Prestian**
   Chief Executive Officer, Owner
   Prestian Corporation

THE NEXT TWO hours fly by preparing for the user group meetings and developing the presentation for the simulation sessions. Renee peeks in. "Kate, the caterers have arrived. I set them up in the conference room. Is there anything else you need for the meeting? If not, I'm going to take a walk over the lunch hour. It's such a beautiful day."

"Go for a walk... we will be fine. I can't imagine we need anything else," I say, heading into the bathroom to brush my teeth and reapply lip gloss. I have to admit it's very nice having a bathroom adjacent to the office.

I walk into the conference room and don't know why I'm so surprised. Chase has arranged this, after all. The conference room table has been removed and replaced with a smaller one, which has been arranged in the center of the room with a tablecloth, napkins, silverware, and glasses. A catered lunch is laid out along one side of the room, and water and fresh lemons are floating in a glass punch dispenser. The silver buffet servers contain salmon with a caramelized glaze, halibut in a creamy dill sauce, seasoned green beans and a cauliflower dish. A small glass bowl displays the reds, oranges and green colors of a mango relish and another holds a salad with a multitude of seasonal garnishes and the dressings are arranged at the end of the table in glass dispensers. I'm not sure if I am ever going to get used to his lifestyle.

"Kate, it feels like ages since I've seen you," Jenny says, announcing her entrance, and as I turn I'm crushed into her arms with a big hug.

"I know, way too long," I say, laughing at my best friend's exuberance. "It's been a crazy week, that's for certain. Luckily most of the drama has blown over now. Chase still has security pretty tight, but at least we're able to return to the city. He had Mom flown back to Naples yesterday. Chase had a meeting scheduled until noon, so he'll be here as soon as he can," I say.

"Hey, before he gets here—I seriously need some updated makeup and could use some more dress skirts and a pair of new fall boots. Would you like to go shopping?"

"Well, I guess you could absolutely drag me. You know how much I hate shopping!" she says.

I laugh. It's so good to see her. "One more thing before Chase arrives. He asked me to go back to Aruba with him at the end of the month. We would leave a little early around three in the afternoon on Wednesday and be back the following Tuesday," I explain.

"Go, Kate, you know you don't have to ask me," she says.

"If you're sure. The Medical Center project is coming along really well. The initial ground soil tests came back good. Terry has plenty of space to work with given the amount of land Chase bought, so there's no concern about needing to constrain the footprint in that regard. I just finished the load leveling schedule and data for the exam room capacity. I feel confident we won't have to overbuild. The simulation should demonstrate that clinicians will have three exam rooms available for use when practicing, but that we don't have to build three per clinician. This should save us a few million dollars alone based on the square footage," I explain.

"Glad to hear it," Chase says as he walks across the conference area. He extends his hand to Jenny. "Jenny, happy to see you again, and this time under better circumstances," he says.

"Good to see you too, Chase. I recall the last time we were together you were quite frantic with worry," she says. I smile at her graciousness. Grumpy, bossing and overbearing are my recollections of him while I was in the hospital. The poor nurse and doctors.

"Lunch smells great, and I'm hungry. Why don't we get something to eat and then we can talk," he says, waving us towards the buffet. "It was catered by Zambia's. The food is always good, they have a variety of options, and a way of making even the starkest conference room look like an excellent little restaurant," he says.

"It was sweet of you to invite me, Chase," Jenny says as we sit with our lunch. "Kate and I haven't seen each other in longer than normal. I suspect you're keeping her pretty busy," she says, then blushes as we both look at her, clearly thinking the same thing.

"Katarina is somewhat of a workaholic, so I'm trying to get her not to work as much, actually," Chase explains, steering clear of the inference.

"I've been telling her to quit working so much for years, Chase. Maybe you'll have more success," she says.

"How did this conversation end up being about me? I just like to make sure everything is done, and all the details are in place," I say, scowling my displeasure before taking another bite of the salmon topped with mango salsa.

"Speaking of the hours Katarina works. That is a perfect segue into why I asked you both to have lunch with me. We've had previous discussions about the Chicago Medical Centers and the fact that we've purchased land for two buildings. The contract we currently have in place is for the initial bid and subsequent work involving one facility, which means we still need to amend the contract between Prestian and Torzial to include both and the work required to get the projects to design."

"Chase, you're paying us for the development of the patient experience and the design as a result of that work. In this particular case it just happens the future state called out the need for two locations and renegotiating the contract never came into my mind, " she says.

"Well, renegotiating my contract is never far from Chase's mind," I blurt.

"Kate, he has a point. Maybe that's why you've needed to put in so many hours," Jenny says.

"One might think so, but actually, I've spent most of my time to this point on the one facility, working through exam room data and simulation. The providers, as in most cases, are worried about how many exam rooms they will have. I'm confident the angst will subside after the presentation and simulation," I explain.

"Jenny, I didn't bring up the multiple facilities to make you feel bad about Katarina's hours, but instead to have a discussion about the future. She is currently putting in long hours, merely working on one design and hasn't even moved from the primary care practice flows into the other social services, pharmacy or medical assistance services the new center will offer. A lot of that is her drive to do an excellent job and accomplish targets. However, I'd like to have an open dialogue about expanding our scope and business relationship. Typically, I would have worked with you directly, but given the fact I'm in a relationship with the person I want to hire, and you are best friends, I felt it best to include Katarina in the conversation if that is okay with you," he says.

"Of course it is," she says, not giving away that she knows how angry I was with Chase the last time he talked to her about my assignments without discussing it with me.

"Jenny, the return on investment, specifically the increase in quality of people's health in Chicago and reduction of health care costs, has been staggering in the pilot site, as you know from the data Katarina has provided.

"It's been astonishing," she says.

"Indeed, and given that, additional opportunities exist to close the barriers to healthcare in the inner city. We plan to integrate the care process for Chicago, but in two distinct footprints.

"So far I'm with you, Chase. Kate shared the data with me and it's the right thing to do," Jenny says.

"I would agree. However, I've been asked to assist with another project in Southern Illinois. They need an investor, and I'm interested in backing their efforts. They are highly motivated and ready to change the way they provide care, and it will make a significant difference in the community. I need Torzial, and precisely the knowledge and experience Katarina brings to ensure my investment is sound. I'm not interested, however, in watching Katarina burn out as we expand, nor am I interested in having anyone else manage the process side of Prestian Corp projects," he says.

"You've definitely sparked my interest," Jenny says.

"I have a proposal. Katarina enjoys working with you and has loyalty to your company. You gave her the opportunity, exposure, and experience she needed to become who she is and she's happy working for Torzial. The reality is that I will be called on to back more medical centers financially, and they will all become part of Prestian Medical Center Enterprises. I want Katarina to manage the designs and efficiencies in these facilities, but she can't do it alone."

"It definitely sounds like a large undertaking," Jenny says.

"I'm proposing Torzial branch out and develop a division specifically dedicated to Prestian Medical Center. I would leave it up to you and Katarina to develop a structure for the department including the hiring and training of staff. At the end of the day, I want Katarina in charge of any Prestian Medical Center initiative and to have an organizational structure which provides resources to accomplish it. If we can develop that, I'd like to talk about the exclusivity of contract," he says.

"Chase, I think it makes perfect sense given your expansion desires and Katarina's abilities. But, need I point out the obvious. You have plenty of money, and Katarina would work on anything you asked her to. Why do you want to keep Torzial in the contract?" she asks, taking a sip of her water.

"Jenny, you have a great business, and I'm most definitely interested in making sure it thrives given my personal relationship with Katarina. I am also a very selfish man, Jenny. These facilities will most certainly be nationwide as we expand. The builds and commitments for each are at least a year, if not two years in duration. I'm not interested in having Katarina committed to that extent. I would rather she have an organizational structure that ensures the process work is done in the same efficient and profitable manner for each site, but without doing all the work herself.

"I see," Jenny says, glancing in my direction.

"I know this is a lot to consider. I've taken the liberty of looking into the financial health of Torzial. It's small but has been remarkably successful. You've invested wisely, which helped protect you during the recession, and as a result, your firm has been able to provide many people with great jobs. I'm extremely impressed with the benefits package you offer your staff. It's clear you care about the welfare of your employees, and that's something I respect a great deal."

"Thank you, Chase," she says.

"I would envision needing to at least triple the size of your company, as we expand nationally. I know you've done well financially and saved well, but an expansion of this magnitude will be costly. We'll write the expense into the initial startup, and you have my word you will have a very lucrative contract. The finances of the expansion should be your last concern. The more pressing question is does going national interest you?" he asks.

"The excitement you and Kate have for this project is contagious. Increasing quality of health care and driving down its costs is a national issue and I would be proud to have Torzial a part of it. I'd like to hear what Kate thinks about the proposal, though. She's undeniably great at her job, but more importantly, she's my best friend, and that relationship means a great deal to me," she says.

"Jenny, just so we're clear... Chase and I did not talk about this before today. I am as shocked by the proposal as you probably are. I would like nothing better than to see the healthcare delivery system redesigned one community at a time and having it roll out under the Prestian Medical Center name would be exciting. Chase is right, though, I couldn't handle this magnitude alone. It's your call, though, Jenny."

"I'm admittedly enthusiastic about the expansion opportunities, but there is one thing. I don't ever want to lose the Torzial name. The company was started with the money my dad left me when he passed away. It's his legacy to my future family and me," she says.

"Jenny, Torzial is a company to be proud of. The names of the divisions or subsidiaries are completely up to you. Why don't the two of you start working on an organizational structure? I'll have our attorneys begin drafting a contract that we can discuss and modify as we move through this."

"Chase, I think we should toast to a future partnership," she says, lifting her glass of water. I'm appreciative of the offer and the chance to expand. Kate and I will start working on putting a proposal together and let you know when we have it prepared for your review."

"Sounds like a plan. Unfortunately, since I've been out of the office for a few days, I need to return to another meeting. I'll leave you ladies to discuss the logistics. Just let me know when you want to meet. He extends a hand to Jenny. "It's been a pleasure getting to know you a little better and I'm looking forward to working with you and your company in the future," he says.

"Katarina, I won't be done until about six this evening, but Jay will take you home. He leans over and gives me a chaste kiss on the lips before he departs. I know he is watching to see how I react to his public display of affection. *Two can play this game.*

"Perks to dating the boss," I say in response to Jenny's raised eyebrows and the question in his eyes. His eyes narrow at my comment, and he tries to hide his amusement.

"I'll see you when I get home, Katarina," he says, shaking his head and excusing himself on the way out of the door.

"I have to admit he seems very nice, and I'm not just saying that because he offered to expand Torzial nationally. He actually appears to care about the employees and he's clearly in love with you. He is a little intense, though. Is he always, so, in control of everything?" she asks.

"Jenny, he is always in control of everything. You know, at first, it was annoying, but I seriously don't think I would want him any other way now. He's controlling in a good way. It's hard to explain, but today would be a good example. Ordinarily, I would have been pissed that he didn't ask me my opinion, but he already knew how I felt about my switching companies. He had asked me offhandedly about coming over to Prestian, and I told him I was happy where I was. He wants me to work on his projects; I wouldn't be satisfied working on any other project, and so he proposes a solution that works for everyone. He's seriously an excellent negotiator like that. But to answer your question, he's quite controlling, no doubt about it."

"It's none of my business, but you seemed to have worked through your concerns about dating someone in the office," she says.

"We seriously need time to catch up, Jenny. I haven't even had a chance to fill you in on all the stuff that happened with Mom this week. I was serious about getting some new makeup and shopping. You want to go to breakfast on Saturday, and then go shopping? We could even ask the guys if they want to go out for drinks afterward."

"Sounds like a plan. It would be nice if they could get to know each other, too. I'll ask Ty when I get home and text you," she says, giving me a big hug before leaving and I head back to my office.

MESSAGE: Jenny and I are going for breakfast, makeovers and a day of shopping on Sat. We need dates afterward. She's asking Ty. Interested?

> **Reply:** Of course. Make sure Jay has an itinerary by Friday at noon.
> **Message:** It's a date!
> **Reply:** What no argument?
> **Message:** No, I'm getting used to your bizarre requests.
> **Reply:** Careful, Baby. I do know where your office is.

I SMILE at his last comment and turn my attention to the work at hand. The afternoon is filled pulling process slides together into a concise, comprehensive presentation. The desk phone buzzes and I hit the speaker phone, still concentrating on the screen in front of me. "Kate, I have Dalton Hayes, CEO of Houston Medical Center on the line for your four o'clock meeting," Renee announces. The conference lasts the entire hour, reviewing metrics and return on investment. Hayes agrees to do a short video clip on the Houston model redesign efforts including outcomes that Torzial can use in presentations going forward. I enter a slide as a placeholder for his clip noting some of the detail in our conversation, feeling excited about the outcomes.

I sense his presence and look up to find him watching me with deep, intense green eyes and a firmly set jaw. "What's the matter?" I ask, detecting his agitation.

"Katarina, you were supposed to be downstairs with Jay at four thirty. He called to let me know you hadn't arrived and were still here. They adjusted the security detail to accommodate the change but don't have a clue what your plans are. Why are you still here?" he asks.

"I had a conference call from four to five... I didn't see it on my calendar earlier. We actually got a commitment from Hayes to do a video clip about the project outcomes," I explain.

"I'm happy for you, but more interested in getting you to take your security detail seriously," he states.

"I'm sorry, the schedule changed, and I just got busy," I explain, irritated that he's upset about something so trivial.

"Katarina, it's not something you can forget. It's the most important thing you do, keep security appraised of what you're doing so they can do their job."

"I'm sorry they were worried, but seriously, they know I'm here, you see I'm here, so why are you upset?" I ask more than slightly annoyed now.

"What if I came into your office and you weren't here, Katarina?" he asks tightly.

"You are overreacting, Chase. I know you are only protecting me, and I'll try to remember, but seriously... I need a little space," I say.

"You need to give me your word that you're going to take this seriously going forward. You can decide to agree or argue, but we both know how that will end," he says with a hint of a smile.

"Ahh... so you want to play?" I ask affably. "That sounds like much more fun than arguing," I say, running my finger across my upper lip.

"Whatever the lady feels appropriate for the multitude of transgressions I'm sure could be accommodated," he says evenly. His tone is serious, but I see the spark in his eye.

"Maybe we should go home and discuss options in a warm bubble bath with a glass of wine," I say, feeling myself moistening with anticipation.

"You need only ask once, Katarina. The meeting I was staying late to attend has canceled so we can go back to Prestian tonight," he says, carrying my bags and guiding me toward the elevator.

The car ride home is filled with sexual energy. Chase has his arm loosely around my shoulders and his fingers rubbing in a circular pattern along the side of my neck are sending goosebumps down my arms. He's quiet, reticent and clearly still agitated. Jay pulls up to the front door to let us out when we arrive, and Matt unloads our belongings.

We are alone in our room, and I can't quite make out the emotion in his eyes... something guarded. He pulls me into his arms crushing me to him, capturing my lips roughly, expertly parting my lips to allow his tongue passage. I'm breathless, as he finally pulls his mouth from mine, but keeps me pressed tightly against his rock hard crotch.

"Baby, you drive me absolutely crazy. I'd like to spank your beautiful little ass red right now," he says breathlessly.

"When have you ever needed permission," I ask, feeling the desire building just at the thought.

"Baby, your lack of sexual inhibition is such a turn on," he says, pressing his mouth against mine. "I want to fuck you in our bed... right now," he says. His hands glide up my thighs, slowly skimming the lacy edge of my panties before sliding them down over my heels. His fingers tease the soft hair between my legs before he explores lower, sliding his finger in the sensitive area. "Baby, you're already so wet," he says, gliding the lubrication across my clit, pressing softly with every caress.

"Please, don't stop," I murmur, pushing up to grind against his touch.

"Hold still, Baby, I want you to feel every stroke," he says, continuing the pattern then slowing moving his finger away.

"Don't stop, Chase," I murmur.

"Patience."

He takes his time, letting his tongue explore the insides of my thighs, brushing through the soft hair, teasing me with his warm wet tongue connects with my clit, again. I push against him... unable to control the squirming.

"There now... be still Katarina or I will spank you tonight," he says before sliding his tongue over my clit again, maintaining his rhythm until I can no longer hold back my release and tremble around him. He captures my clit between his lips sucking hard, claiming all I have to give.

"Baby, I want to see your beautiful ass in the air," he says, positioning me face down on the bed and pulling me up at the waist. His pants fall to the floor, and he pulls me closer to the edge of the bed slowly rubbing his cock around my ass.

"I can't get enough of you. I want to bury myself deep inside of you. Ready, Baby? I want to fuck you hard and fast," he says, plunging into me, grasping my hips as we begin to gain momentum. He's rubbing against that special spot inside of me, and I feel myself start to build again.

"Honey," I moan, arching my back when he pushes in, gaining momentum and driving in deeper and faster.

"Katarina, cum with me, " he urges as he plunges deep inside of me, bringing me to the edge as we release the day's tension and emotion together. I collapse, and he pulls me into his arms. I can hear the steady and viral beat of his heart as I lay against his chest.

"I could listen to your heartbeat all night... I love you," I whisper.

"I love you, too, Baby. I don't think you have any idea what you mean to me," he says, pushing the hair out of my eyes and holding me tight against his chest.

"You were so mad at me," I say accusingly.

"Correction, I'm still mad that you don't put yourself and your security first," he says, but it's because I love you, and I worry about you."

"I'll try to do a better job of keeping them apprised when I'm not with you, although it's not really very often," I say, running my fingers through the dark hair on his chest.

"That's the way I like it," he says.

"Such a control freak… you're just lucky I find it a little romantic when you take charge."

"Romantic, huh?" he says, raising his eyebrows. "Maybe I should be a little bit more controlling… then you might actually listen."

"I thought you were going to spank me tonight," I say, pretending to pout.

"Baby, I love spanking you and watching your body's response. I enjoy how wet it makes you, but I was too upset with you to do that, Katarina," he says.

"Oh, that mad?" I say.

"That upset, Katarina. Security, it's your number one job. Okay?" he says, kissing me on the nose. I lean down to check an incoming text.

Message: Where are we meeting tomorrow?

"I better let Jenny know plans," I say.

He slides off the bed and reaches into the pocket of his suit jacket still lying carelessly over the chair and pulls out a card, handing it to me. "I was going to give this to you tomorrow morning… but, since you're making plans," he says.

I open the envelope and pull out a gift card. It's a Courtier LeBien spa certificate.

"I've taken the liberty of making reservations for you and Jenny. The gift card will cover whatever you and Jenny want in the way of makeovers, hair, and spa treatments," he says.

"Chase, you didn't have to do this, but it means a lot that you went out of your way organizing a special day for us to spend time together."

The certificate looks expensive with raised lettering and insignia. I reach for the card inside the envelope and read the note written on the card.

KATARINA:

Please accept this gift as nothing more than it is… a gift certificate for the woman I am in love with and her best friend to have an incredible day of makeup, hair, spa and shopping.

Love,

Chase

Enclosed in the pocket of the card is a Visa card. I pull the card out, and there's nothing to indicate the amount or anything on the card.

"Chase, what is this?"

"It's an open account, Katarina. I want you and Jenny to shop on the Mile where you might not otherwise shop and buy whatever you like."

"Chase, Honey, this is too much. The makeover was kind, but I make great money. I might not be able to afford to shop in the Mile district, but I can afford to buy my own clothes," I exclaim.

"Katarina, I want to spend money on you and buy you gifts. It makes me happy to be able to provide for you," he says, clearly irritated with the conversation.

"I can provide for myself, though. It's enough that you won't take money for rent, food, utilities or anything. I'm sorry. I know you are only trying to be nice, but..."

"You are my partner, and I want to provide for you. What is so wrong with that?" he asks, his dark green eyes capturing mine.

"I don't know, Chase. The gift of a make-over is one thing, but an open account to buy clothes? The price for one skirt at most of those stores is more than most people make in a week. I don't need clothes that cost that much," I explain.

"Katarina, I don't know how to get past your reluctance to let me provide for you. Go with Jenny; buy a couple fun dresses for the evenings in Aruba, matching shoes, and whatever else you need. The card is good for both of you. I'm going to get a little work done before dinner," he says, sliding a pair of jeans on.

Why can't I just accept his gift without feeling like it's payment for sex? He's never done anything to make me feel like that. Jenny will be able to help.

I feel like such a heel as he heads downstairs.

Message: I need to talk to you.

Reply: Call me... I'm free.

Message: k

. . .

I CLICK ON HER NUMBER, and she answers immediately. "Jenny... I feel terrible. Chase gave us this incredible package for tomorrow. A spa day at Courtier LeBien on the Mile. I was so touched that he wanted to arrange a time for us to be able to spend time together. Then on the same card, there's an open account to go buy clothes. I told him I didn't want it or him buying my clothes. He's clearly upset."

"Kate, I think you're reading way too much into this. He wants to buy you some nice clothes and for you to have a splendid time. I admit, I was a little unsure about him at first, but anyone can see he's crazy about you. He clearly respects your talents, or he wouldn't have renegotiated the entire Torzial relationship. He seems like a great guy, and it's not his fault he's wealthy. Those things don't define a man; it's how he treats you and from what I've seen he treats you like a friggin princess," she says.

"He does, and I probably overreacted, but I just don't know how to reconcile the fact he won't let me pay rent, help with utilities, food or anything. He pays for absolutely everything," I say.

"If you moved in with someone that didn't have a ton of money, but wanted to take care of all the bills, wouldn't you find that admirable?"

"God, you're right, Jenny. I would probably think it was more than admirable," I say.

"I personally believe that you should tell him you're sorry for being such a shit, we should go have a spa day and shop the hell out of the Mile," she exclaims laughing.

"Leave it to you to put this into perspective! Let's meet for break-fast at Spazzia's around eight tomorrow morning," I say, hanging up and now anxious to find Chase.

He is on the phone, and I turn so as not to disturb him, but he points to the seat next to him. "Sid, it's going to be different this time. The negotiations are going to be in our own back yard, not overseas. We'll meet the resistance of politicians, lobbyist groups, and every pharmaceutical company in the nation as we expand. It's a good model and Houston is already seeing significant outcomes. Katarina has a video clip that will demonstrate the model's improvements, and specif-ically how Houston has been able to reduce its health care costs as a result," he says, pausing to listen to the person on the line.

"No, we'll plan to release it after the Prestian facilities here and in lower Illinois have State approval. Once that video goes public the entire Prestian project will be of interest. They'll be knocking down your door to get press conferences, interviews and specifically trying to pin down intentions for expansion. Okay, thanks, Sid," he says, disconnecting.

"Chase, I didn't realize creating the video would be a detriment to our project," I state.

"It's not, Katarina. It's impactful and should be shared. We just need to manage the timing," he says, pushing the hair out of my eyes.

"I'm sorry I overreacted to the shopping gift, Chase. It was a very nice thing to do, and I don't mean to seem ungrateful. Sometimes, I just feel like I don't contribute anything. I know you didn't intend it as anything but a thoughtful gift, but I don't want to feel like I am being kept," I say, reaching up to kiss his lips.

"Baby, we've talked about this before. You are my partner; I want to provide for you. I was just trying to give you a beautiful day. But, I'm sure there's some just punishment for such a headstrong young lady," he says, grinning wickedly.

NINE

PRESTIAN

I wake up excited to see Jenny on Saturday morning. It's just turned five a.m. so plenty of time for a nice long run and a shower. Chase is at the kitchen table in gym clothes and studying something on his MacBook, but looks up as I come down the stairs.

"Hi Baby," he says, his eyes slowly taking in my attire. "You're going out for a run?"

"I am, and you'll be happy to know that I texted Jay yesterday," I say surprised Jay wouldn't have already told him.

"Are you taking the lake path?" he asks.

I groan... "Chase, I have reflectors on my clothes." I put my jacket on, zip it up and twirl around for him. "See... I have two strips on the back and two on the front. It's the newest design by Patagonia," I declare smugly.

"I see you are quite reflective," he says, with an amused grin.

"I'll have you know that my shoes are quite bright and visible, too. People can't help but see me a mile away, now will you please stop worrying?"

"I'd much prefer you run on the treadmill this time of year, but I will admit you seem to have taken precautions, so I'll try not to worry," he says as Jay walks in the room.

"We're all set, Kate," he says, nodding to Chase.

"Did they install the lights on the lake path, yet, Jay?" Chase asks.

"They installed them a couple days ago when you asked about them," he replies, smiling and shaking his head good-naturedly at Chase.

"Good," Chase responds to Jay.

I narrow my eyes at him.

"I'm going to head back to the city and work for a while. There are a few things that came up overnight I need to attend to. Jay will fly you into the city when you're ready and I'll meet you later at Bazil's," he says, kissing me lightly on the lips. "Oh, and text me when you get home from your run and enjoy your day with Jenny."

Message: Just in from my run. The lights were fantastic!

Reply: Glad you like them.

Message: You lit up the entire lake path! You're incorrigible!!

Reply: Probably...

Message: See you at Bazil's.

WE GET INTO THE HELICOPTER, and I laugh as Jay hands me a set of earplugs, looking slightly embarrassed. He smiles apologetically. "Sorry Kate, bosses orders," he says, as I put them on before pulling on my headphones and we lift off towards the city.

Jay assists me out of the helicopter into the awaiting limo, and it's a short drive to Spazzia's which is a quiet little coffee shop renowned for its Italian Crème. I spot Jenny at a table towards the back. "Have you been here long?" I ask, taking the chair opposite her.

"No, I only beat you by a few moments. So, I'm dying to know how your conversation went," she says.

"I apologized, and we're okay, but he didn't press me to use the card after that."

The waitress arrives, and we both order a flavored coffee. "He made reservations for us at The Courtier Le Bien at ten a.m. so we have plenty of time to catch up. So, tell me what's going on with Ty. I didn't know it had progressed to the point of you wanting to move in with him," I say, smirking.

"Well, we haven't officially moved in together, but I usually end up staying most nights with him. His condo is close to his office, and it actually takes me less time to get to the office from his place.

"You seem happy. I'm excited for you," I say, taking in the sparkle in her eyes.

"Me, too. You know it just sort of happened," she says, smiling.

"I don't know how Chase and I came about so quickly either." The waitress circles back with oversized ceramic mugs steaming with the aroma of freshly brewed coffee. I inhale the scent of delicious roasted hazelnut in my own, and Jenny slips a spoon in hers to sample a few of the chocolate shavings that are sprinkled on her drink.

"I love being at Prestian, but I really do miss the Torzial fun, too. It's just the office at Prestian saves me so much time running around town, and hauling stuff," I say.

"Yeah, and he's right around the corner," she says, and we both burst out laughing. We spend another hour catching up on all the drama of the week before we get ready to leave the coffee shop.

The Courtier Le Bien is not far away, and we arrive in plenty of time for our reservations. A eucalyptus infused steam room first, a mineral oil pool, manicure and pedi, and then makeup is on the agenda. I explain to the technician that I don't wear a lot of makeup and am just looking for a little warmer look for fall. She applies a light mineral powder, some matte neutral and brown tone eye shadow, a brown copper colored liner just to the lower lids and finishes with a light brown coat of mascara. "Let me add just a little blush and a soft apricot lip gloss," she says, applying her finishing touches.

Jenny, being a brunette, went with vibrant colors for fall and winter. I can see them looking fabulous with her extensive collection of colorful scarfs.

"Do you like it?" I ask.

"Yes, I just hope Ty likes it," she giggles.

"I know he will. Could we both have one of everything?" I ask the technician.

"Most certainly," she says, leaving to package our makeup.

"Kate, you've lost your mind; that stuff must be a small fortune. I'll pay for my own makeup," she says.

"Oh, no you don't. He said the gift was for both of us to enjoy, so dammit that's exactly what we're going to do," I exclaim bound and determined not to let Jenny off the hook. "Hair next... we have to look hot for our dates tonight," I say. The stylists set to work on our styles. Jenny settles on a minimal trim to her long chestnut-colored hair with some layers around her face. The technician suggests leaving my length, adding a few longer layers of movement, thinning out the bulk, and adding highlights that will catch the light and give it a coppery sheen. Kate and I are talking so much I lose track of time.

"What do you think?" the stylist asks, turning me around.

I stare at my hair in the mirror. "I absolutely love it. It seems so tame and glossy, so unlike the unruly hair I'm used to dealing with. How can I get it to look like this every day?" I ask.

"I'll send you home with a little product which should be applied before drying it straight," she says, running through a list of products and what each does. We leave the store laughing at the absurd amount of product we will now be applying to our hair each morning.

"It really was very thoughtful that he wanted us to have a girl's day without worrying about price. I still feel sorry that I reacted like that. I think we need to find a lingerie store... the hot stuff," I add.

"I know just the place," she says, laughing. "Bella Bonita... it's where you go when you want hot lingerie that most people can't even think about affording," she says.

"I'll text Chase and see if we can ditch security and have a little privacy."

Message: How do I lose the security for a short while?

Reply: You don't. Why?

Message: Pout... It's a surprise! For you!

Reply: Losing security is not an option. Text Jay. He can tell you what can be accommodated.

Message: Pouting....

Message: Jenny and I need privacy at the next store. How? Chase said text you...

Reply: Tell me where.

Message: Bella Bonita...

Reply: Yep, we'll go in first. When you see us come out together, you can go in.

Message: You're the best!!

Reply: Change of plans. Stay outside until I text you.

Message: Okay. What's wrong?

Reply: There's a back door that leads into the alley. Give us a minute to get someone posted.

Message: Thanks, Jay. Sorry for the bother.

Reply: No worries. You can go in now.

"I'm pretty sure you can do some damage in this store. It's where all the elite shop," Jenny says as we enter the boutique. It is filled with delicate lingerie of the finest fabric and styles, modeled on mannequins with exquisitely shaped bodies.

"Wow, I think that would be right up Chase's alley," I say, fingering the luxurious silk of the high cut thong bottoms and sheer lace top.

"And what about this," she says, holding up a sheer red nightgown that leaves little to the imagination.

"I'm pretty sure it wasn't designed to bend over in," I say, holding its length against my frame.

"Funny. I'm pretty sure it was intended for just that purpose," Jenny says, laughing while she holds up a couple more.

"Sold. I think I'll wear one of the sets tonight, but save the others for Aruba. Pick a few for yourself," I say.

"Absolutely not."

"Jenny, you were the one that said it wasn't a big deal for him to want us to enjoy ourselves. Pick or I will select for you and you know my taste is not nearly as good as yours," I threaten.

"Okay, okay, you're right. In fact, I think this little number in a black and white will do quite nicely, " Jenny says laughing.

"Total hottie! Ty is going to love them!" I say as we pay for our merchandise and leave the store.

THE AFTERNOON FLIES by as we roam Michigan Avenue taking in the new fall designs. "Does the security team always stay this close to you?" Jenny asks.

"Always. It takes a while to get used to, but I couldn't imagine being without them now. It is a little odd that Jay is with us in addition to Matt and Sheldon. He's usually with Chase if we are apart. I'll have to ask him about that a little later," I say. The boutique on the corner catches our eye, and I spot a short, fitted, rust-colored dress for the evening.

"What do you think?" I ask, holding it up to me.

"Hot," she says.

"Here, try it on with these, she says holding up a pair of outrageous heels.

"Jenny, you know I like my flat sandals," I protest and groan in mock despair.

"Yeah, but these will make you look so sexy... just try them on," she encourages.

It's the perfect fall dress; long sleeves to provide a little cover, short, but not too short, and would look good with sandals, flats, heels, or boots. I slide it over my head and am excited that it fits perfectly. The rust color is a beautiful compliment to my coloring and the patterns in the material remind me of fall. I grimace at the patent leather brown Louboutin pumps, but sit down to put them on and fasten the straps around my ankles. Jeez, they must be almost four inches high. I look in the mirror and have to admit they look great with the dress. I come out of the dressing room, and Jenny nods her approval. "Yes, that outfit is totally hot. I bet you end up in bed with your heels on tonight," she says.

"Jenny!" I exclaim...

"What... just keeping it real. You really don't think so?" she says.

"I'm almost positive I would lose," I concede, smiling at her exuberance.

"If we hurry, we'll have just enough time to stop by our place and change before we meet the guys," I suggest.

"Jay, would you mind running us by the condo? We're going to change before we meet the guys at Bazil's," I explain as we get back into the limousine.

"Not a problem at all, Kate," he says, pulling out in the bumper to bumper traffic. He navigates the city blocks, and we are soon back at the high-rise. He greets the doorman who offers to have the bellboy assist with the packages, but Jay lets him know that he will take them himself.

"Is Chase still at the office?" I ask, riding up in the elevator.

"Yes, he's been working all day, but he's leaving shortly and will meet you at the restaurant."

Message: Just arrived. Give them your name and they will escort you to our table.

Reply: We're at the condo changing. Be about 15 minutes.

Message: Jay is with you?

Reply: Yes, stop worrying!

Message: BTW why is he with us today?

He doesn't respond and I scowl at the phone, but look up when Jenny walks out of the bathroom. "You look fabulous," I praise.

"Thanks," she says, twirling around.

"The peach color is beautiful and the sweater material looks so soft," I say.

"What do you think about the black boots with this?" she asks.

"You're really asking me about style?" I ask laughing.

"On second thought," she says.

"Hey," I say, pretending to pout.

"Just kidding. I'm going to touch up the makeup a little bit and I'll be ready to go," Jenny says, walking towards the bathroom while I head for the bedroom. I change into one of my newly purchased bra and panty sets. The bra is white with a sheer lace cup, and the thong style panties make me feel a little risqué as I quickly pull the new dress over my head. I buckle the dainty straps around my ankles and grimace at the heels as I stand up. I sincerely hope I don't fall in the damn things tonight. I find Jenny in the living room ready to go.

"Whoa... look at you! Chase is one lucky man," she exclaims warmly.

"I hope he likes it," I say slightly embarrassed by my friend's enthusiasm. "And you look absolutely amazing! I can't wait to see the look on Ty's face when he catches sight of you walking in," I say.

"I'm excited to see him tonight. He's been traveling the past week, and I feel like we've barely seen each other," she says.

"Chase has a table reserved under his name if you want to let Ty know."

The restaurant is a short distance from the condo and Jay slides into the passenger seat up front while the driver quickly navigates traffic, pulling up in front of an elite looking club that already has lines gathering at the entrance. Jay opens my door, and the driver does likewise for Jenny, escorting us efficiently through the crowd and towards the hostess, letting her know we are with the Prestian party. We're promptly joined by another hostess who ushers us through to the back of the establishment. Chase and Ty are talking at a bar overlooking the water. They look comfortable with each other and have already ordered a drink.

Chase looks up as we make our way towards them and the smoldering look he gives me tells me he approves of the outfit. His dark green eyes take in every detail of the dress, lingering on my exposed thighs and traveling up every inch of my body before capturing my eyes with his. *Oh, my... with that look, I don't think we'll be out very late.*

He puts his arm around me. "Baby, you look fabulous. I'm going to have a hard time keeping my hands off of you until later," he whispers. I look up, and Ty is whispering something that only Jenny can hear, and I give her a mischievous smile and a wink. Chase and Ty guide us to our table and hold our chairs out for us while we are seated. I can't help think how lucky we are to have such gentlemen for dates.

"Ty and I have been getting to know each other a little better while we were waiting for you," Chase says.

Jenny and I both look up questioningly. "It seems we have many of the same business associates and friends. We've actually been introduced to each other on several occasions," he explains.

"Small world," Jenny says smiling.

The guys have started with a local micro-brewery beer. "What would you two like to drink?" Chase asks.

Jenny and I smile. "Cranberry Vodka, please," I reply laughing.

"Something we should know about?" Chase asks, his eyebrows raised in question.

"We went out several years ago for a ladies night, and a few of our friends were having these drinks. We tried them, a lot of them... since then, when we're out together it's our drink of choice... that's all," Jenny explains.

"We can be pretty fun once we've had one or two of these to drink," she adds, winking at Ty. "We must have danced until one or two in the morning," she says recalling our escapade.

The waitress brings our drinks, and the guys order another beer and appetizers for everyone. The view from our table is overlooking Lake Michigan to one side and not far from the dance floor.

"I'm happy that Chase and Ty are getting along so well. I was a little apprehensive. It would be kind of awkward if our boyfriends didn't get along or want to spend time together," Jenny says to me while the men are talking.

Chase leans over and touches my elbow as the sound of sultry and jazzy melody floods the establishment. "If you'll excuse us," Chase says to Jenny and Ty before leading me to the dance floor. He holds me close, letting me follow his lead and acclimate to the steps.

"Baby, I couldn't wait any longer to have you in my arms," he whispers. The music is slow, sultry, yet pulsing and vibrant. As the song ends, Chase unfolds me from his arms but keeps a steady hand on mine as he begins dancing to the pulsating rhythm, guiding me with him to the beat. *God, he's sexy.* The music is hot, and we dance to a few more songs before he leads me winded from the floor. As we reach our table, the waitress brings us both a fresh drink. I see that Ty and Jenny are dancing now.

"Take another sip; I want to get you back on the dance floor. The waitress will be bringing out our meal in another twenty-five minutes, or so. I took the liberty of placing an order when I booked the reservation since you're not the best about pacing yourself," he says. I can't help but laugh at his controlling tendencies.

"Are you always going to take care of my every need?" I ask, smiling.

His eyes rise in response, and he guides me to the dance floor, his hand on the small of my back. The music is pulsing and energetic, and somehow I manage to keep up to the beat of the music. I look up, and Jenny and Ty have made their way over to us, keeping a perfect rhythm together. The band switches to a slower more sultry sound and Chase pulls me into his arms for this dance.

"Baby, that's how we're going to make love tonight... fast and then slow... I'm going to bring us to the very brink, and then we're going to stay there....right on the edge," he whispers, holding me close as he guides me around the dance floor. When the song ends, Ty and Chase guide us back to our table which has been laden with fresh chicken salads, flatbread and a glass carafe filled water and fresh lemons. I notice that my drink has disappeared, and I look up at Chase. He is smiling at me.

Message: Pace and patience...

Reply: I'm having fun! Bring my drink back!

Message: You'll have more fun if the night lasts longer... Trust me!

Reply: Control freak!

Message: Yes, ma'am...

"Kate, Jenny tells me you are responsible for the design of the Houston Medical Center complex," Ty says as we eat.

"Well, I was the facilitator for the design group, but it was the team that really did the work. I'm excited to see what the architects will come up with," I say.

"Chase and I were talking about the project a little before you arrived. It'll be great for the city of Chicago if the Prestian Medical Centers do as well," Ty says.

The waitress comes around to remove our dinner and Chase orders a round of drinks for everyone.

"If you two don't mind, I'm going to steal my date away for a little dance before our drinks arrive," Chase says.

"Looks like a few reporters in the corner," he says, pulling me close and leading me to a rather slow and sultry beat. The raw sensual tension between us is almost electric. I feel his penetrating gaze and look into his smoldering deep green eyes. He pushes the hair out of my eyes, holding me close as we dance to the music.

The drinks have arrived by the time we return to our table and Jenny and I laugh at how quickly they vanish. She orders two more, and we reminisce about the first night we went out drinking together while Ty and Chase are in conversation. It vaguely reminds me how bad my head hurt the next day, and I sip this one a little slower. Chase touches my elbow as he excuses us from the table. "They always play this number close to the end, and it's one of my favorites," he says, wrapping me in his arms as we reach the dance floor.

He seems oblivious to the reporters and draws me close, so my head is resting on his chest. I can feel the sound of his heartbeat over the beat of the music. The sexual tension is palpable.

"Take me home," I whisper as the band finishes the last song and they say thanks to the crowd for coming out. As he leads me back to the table, he stops to shake hands with the band members letting them know what an excellent job they did and how much we enjoyed their music. It always amazes me how much humility the man has for someone in his position. He takes out his phone and texts someone before guiding me over to the reporters' table. He shakes hands with each of them and exchanges pleasantries until we reach Nate, who for whatever reason, seems to be Chase's favorite.

"Good evening, Nate. I trust you were able to get the photographs you needed?" he asks.

"Yes, Mr. Prestian. I was planning to write a small story to submit to the Mid-Western column if there's no opposition," he explains.

"No opposition at all, Nate. You always do a superb job. Let me know if you need anything else. Oh, and get a hold of me the week after next," he says, handing him a business card. "We can discuss some upcoming press releases if you are interested," Chase says.

"I'm definitely interested. Thank you, Mr. Prestian. I'll be in touch."

Jenny hugs me tightly as we say goodnight and Ty assists her to the awaiting car. I see Jay on the driver's side of Chase's Jaguar XJL Ultimate. The drive home is short even in the late evening traffic. We've barely closed the door of our condo before Chase scoops me into his arms and carries me into the bedroom.

"I have one thing on my mind, Baby, and that's to find out what you have on under this dress. Your nipples have been pushing through the material, taunting me all night," he accuses. "Hands in the air now, so I can see what you're wearing," he orders hoarsely. I lift my arms, and he pulls the dress over my waist and head. The intake of breath as he catches sight of my newly purchased bra and panty set makes me blush. He runs his finger over the completely see-through lace netting. "So this is why they were so pointy tonight," he says, rubbing my erect nipples through the lacy material. He turns me, slowly. "Baby, your ass is so perfect, round and muscular; this thong looks amazing on you," he says, cupping my ass in his hands. Bend over the bed and stay there," he instructs as he opens the nightstand. He's clearly positioned me so I can't see what he's doing, and I can already feel myself moistening from the anticipation.

"Baby, I love looking at your perfect ass," he says. I feel completely on display and exposed. *Why does that make me so hot?* I feel his tongue travel along the lines of my panties, across my hips following the line of my thong. It is sensual and intimate. His finger explores the inside of my cheeks, following the thong, before slowly peeling my panties down and letting them drop to the floor.

"Step out of them and lay on the bed face up," he instructs. I do and his finger brushes against my clit, softly beginning to stroke. I arch my hips to increase the friction, but he holds me still. His tongue travels the same pattern, finding my overly aroused clit, while his finger explores the rim of my ass making me writhe with pleasure. "Baby, I want to make you cum over and over tonight," he says, turning me to lay face down on the bed.

"Ready?" he asks.

I am on the brink and can only nod.

"You're going to feel a lubricant, then my fingers and then the same plug we used last week. I need you to tell me if it's too much."

I nod in anticipation, feeling the warm lubricant drizzled between my ass cheeks. Chase rubs it in slowly, exploring, making me needy with want before inserting a finger. I hear myself audibly moan.

"How does that feel, Baby? Is it uncomfortable?" he asks.

"No, it's great, but I don't think I'll last long," I pant.

He lets me acclimate, teasing me and gently stretching me and then begins to stroke my clit before inserting another finger.

"It feels so good, Chase," I moan.

"Slow, Baby, I'm planning to pleasure you for a very long time. If it's too much, tell me," he says as he continues stroking my clit while he slowly works it in past the anal ring. It snaps into place, and he moves it slightly causing me to moan with pleasure.

"I want to feel how wet you are on the end of my cock," he says, standing to remove his clothing before positioning me closer to the edge of the bed. His cock is rock hard, and he rubs it over my clit and all the way down before gently pushing into me. He is slow, patient, as I gasp at the feel of him moving inside of me against the anal plug. It is erotic, and I raise my hips to meet him, but he slows, holding me at the brink, intent on keeping me poised as I feel the pressure building. The fullness from the plug and the weight of his cock pushing against it are suddenly too much.

"Honey," I moan.

"Baby, now; I want to feel you shake on the head of my cock, cum," he urges, and I can no longer hold back racked with spasm after spasm. He finally pulls out of me, watching me intently as his fingers explore the soft hairs between my legs, exposing my now pulsing clit. "I love feeling you shake at the end of my tongue," he says, kissing the most intimate part of my body, pulling the plug at the same time. The feeling is exquisite, and as he begins to suck slightly harder I feel my body start to build again. "Chase, I can't cum again, Honey," I moan.

He doesn't reply but instead pushes the plug in a little deeper at the same time he sucks my captured clit even harder. My body responds of its own accord, shamelessly pushing against his tongue. "That's it, Baby, right on the edge; exactly where I want you," he says, gathering me in his arms as he positions me so that I am straddling his lap. "Those panties make me want to feel my cock deep in your ass. I'm going to remove the plug; when I do, lower yourself onto my cock. You'll be in control of how deep or fast you wish to go," he instructs, leaning back against the large mahogany headrest as he strokes me with his fingers. It is not long before I feel myself begin to build again and push against the feel of his hands between my legs. "You're so hot and wet. Are you ready, Katarina?" he murmurs.

"I am so ready, Honey," I say, arching against him.

"Go as slow as you want, Baby," he says, releasing the plug and lifting me over the top of his body. His hand is on my hips and waist, guiding me as I lower myself onto him, feeling a slight pressure as I pass the widest part of his girth.

"Hold there, Baby. Just feel me inside of you, and let your body adjust. We're in no hurry," he says before capturing my lips with his own.

I am too turned on to speak. I want to feel him all the way inside of me. His eyes are deep and mesmerizing, glazed over with the same passion that I feel.

"Baby, you are almost there... Katarina," he urges, stroking my clit. I moan under his touch, and his eyes are deep stormy seas of desire which makes me lust to please him. I lower myself onto his body and am rewarded with a groan of pleasure.

"Oh, Baby, you have no idea how good that feels," he says, grasping my hips with his free hand. "Slow, Katarina, stay right there for a few moments and get used to the feel. Now, push down slightly," he says, guiding me until he is firmly rooted.

I moan as I acclimate to the feel of him deep inside of me, gently rocking against his finger. I gain as he helps me raise and lower over the top of him. It is intense, and I am unable to continue going slow.

"Good girl, Baby," he says, helping guide my hips as I lower my body faster and deeper. The sound of his voice pushes me over the edge, and I am unable to control the climax that overtakes me, trembling around him as he releases deep inside of me.

He wraps his arms around me, holding me tight to his chest. My body is still full of adrenaline from the intensity, and I slump against him sated and exhausted. "You never cease to amaze me Katarina," he says, kissing my lips while he pushes the strands of hair that have fallen across my face behind my ear.

He takes my hand and leads me to the bathroom and starts the shower. The water is warm, and he begins to soap my body. "So beautiful, Baby," he says, kissing my lips as he changes the direction of the shower to rain over the top of me. I relish in the feel for a few minutes while he makes quick order of showering before we get out. I dry off and slip into my robe, brush my teeth and squeal as he scoops me up from behind and carries me back to bed slipping in beside me.

"How was that for you, Katarina?" he asks, pulling me into his arms.

"It was hot; I didn't expect it to feel so good. I was nervous that you wouldn't fit," I admit blushing.

He kisses my lips long and firmly, pushing the hair out of my eyes. "I fit perfectly. I was made for you, Baby," he says, kissing me again.

"I love you," I murmur and as sleep takes over I vaguely hear him talking, but can't quite make out the words.

I wake and turn over to cuddle up to Chase and realize he's already gone. It's Sunday morning at seven a.m. He runs on such small amounts of sleep. I think it was well after one a.m. before we drifted off. I slip into my running clothes determined to get a long run in by the lake before breakfast. Damn, I forgot to text Jay last night to let him know.

Message: Jay – forgot to text you last night. Ok for a run?

Reply: We're set. Chase thought you might feel like a jog.

Message: Thank you!!

Chase is working on his Mac when I find him sitting at the desk overlooking the city. "I do believe it's Sunday and according to some control freak I know, we are not supposed to be working on Sundays."

He looks mildly amused at my joke. "I see you're ready for a run this morning," he says.

"I forgot to text Jay last night, but he mentioned that you made them aware."

"I did, I assumed you may want to run before we head back to the house. It's a beautiful day; I thought we could take the sailboat out for a while once we get home."

"Sounds amazing," I reply, kissing him before I leave. He seems a little quiet and distant. I can't quite put my finger on it.

TEN

The lakeside park is just starting to wake up with people out walking their dogs, strolling along the lake or running. I hit my playlist and settle into my jog wondering what could be bothering Chase. He was in good spirits last night, and he's not a moody person. I get my breathing down and an hour later slow to a walk where all the vendors are setting up at the entrance to the park. The aroma of freshly brewed coffee and cinnamon pastries wafts through the air. I stop by Charlie's and order black coffee for Chase, a Hazelnut Americano for myself and two pastries to go. As I pay for my purchases, I catch a glimpse of Sheldon by the corner and when I turn around Dereck is in line behind me. He doesn't order but instead follows me as I make my way back to the towers. I greet the doorman and Sheldon pushes the elevator button for me, holding the door for Dereck.

"Is something going on?" I ask as the elevators close.

"We're really not at liberty to discuss security details, Kate. Maybe talk to Chase," he offers apologetically, opening the condo door since my hands are full. I find Chase right where I left him working at the table. Sheldon and Dereck discreetly disappear, and I notice there is a newspaper on the table turned to the Chicago Social Column.

"I stopped and got you a coffee and pastry on the way back," I say.

"Thanks, Baby," he says his eyes softening as they see the concern on my face.

"What's going on Chase? Dereck and Sheldon were glued to me this morning more than normal, and you're clearly preoccupied with something," I add, wondering if it has anything to do with the article lying on the table.

CHICAGO MIDWESTERN

Chase Prestian Spotted at Bazil's

Nate Collins Freelance Journalist

Chase Prestian, multibillionaire and CEO of Prestian Foundation and Holdings danced the night away with Katarina Meilers at Bazil's, the elite nightclub in downtown Chicago last evening. He has been dating Katarina since their business trip to Aruba early last month.

THEY WERE ACCOMPANIED by Ty Channing, legal tycoon and owner of one of the most prestigious financial law firms in the country and his girlfriend Jenny Torzial, sole proprietor of the local Torzial Consulting Firm.

AS THE EVENING ENDED, Chase and Katarina took the time to shake hands and thank members of the local band Destined, renowned for their new edgy, but seductive and sultry sound. Likewise, as he left the club, he made time to personally shake the hands of each paparazzo on site, including yours truly.

THERE DOESN'T SEEM to be anything harmful in the article, but what do I know. I'm still waiting for him to answer. "Chase, what's wrong?" I prompt.

"There's a lot of union unrest right now. We have two of the largest facilities in the Midwest going up right here in the city, in addition to the one pending final sale in the south. The bid package went out, and we've had a barrage of backlash that it's open to everyone. The increased security is just a precaution and need I remind you that you wouldn't have noticed it had you stuck to your course and not stopped for coffee without letting security know."

"I don't know why it surprises me that you know I didn't give them a heads up," I say, annoyed that my every move is reported to him. You've been a little quiet for days. I'm worried about you," I continue.

"It's nothing, Baby, just precautionary," he says reaching for a pastry. I let it drop, but clearly there's more to it than he is letting on.

"The smell of cinnamon and hazelnut was just too tempting after all the exercise I got last night and this morning," I say, sitting down next to him at the table.

"Charlie's?" he asks.

"Yes, they are the best," I say, taking a bite of the warm pastry.

"Don't let Gaby hear you say that," he says laughing.

He seems less apprehensive once we get back home, filling Gaby in with details from the last couple of days while I change clothes, adding a few layers for warmth while we are out on the water. He's apparently planned ahead as the yacht is moored off the dock and Gaby has prepared a large picnic basket of food for us to take along.

It's a perfect fall day to be on the lake, the sun is shining creating a shimmering along the lake. The breeze off the lake is not cold but brisk, with a hint of the long windy Chicago winter to come. Chase takes my hand as we walk toward the dock; there are several men already aboard the long sleek white yacht. It is three stories high and like the one in Aruba, proudly displays the black and gold Prestian crest. Jay, Dereck, and Sheldon are following discreetly behind us.

He introduces the men on the yacht to me as we board and thanks them for their help preparing it. He is in total control as he takes command of the ship. Dereck and Sheldon discreetly disappear somewhere on the boat, while Jay hovers on deck talking to someone on his cell phone. The fact that Chase has more than one yacht does not surprise me given his love for the water. He seems much more relaxed after a few hours navigating the dark blue pristine waters. Shortly after noon, we enjoy the sandwiches, cheese, fruit and little desserts that Gaby packed into the picnic basket and spend the rest of the afternoon discussing wind direction, the differences between port and starboard side and basic rules of boating.

"Here, take the wheel, Baby," Chase says, pulling me from my thoughts. He positions himself behind me and helps me get the feel of it. It takes a little getting used to, but I am exhilarated as we sail across the waters of Lake Michigan.

Gaby has grilled salmon and an arugula salad with caramelized walnuts and goat cheese prepared for dinner. "She's an amazing cook," I say to Chase as I take a sip of the white wine. The crisp finish compliments the meal perfectly, and it feels good to relax after an exhilarating day on the lake.

Chase scowls at an incoming call. "Excuse me, Baby, I need to take this," he says, answering as he heads to his study which is adjacent to the dining room.

I pour myself another glass of white wine and go upstairs. The fresh air was brisk, and I decide to start the whirlpool and relax in its warmth. I pour chamomile scented oil in and inhale its fragrance while I slip out of my clothes and put my hair up in a clip. The water swirls around my body, warming and relaxing. I lie back against the pillow and close my eyes, enjoying the bubbling spa as it circles around me. I am completely relaxed and feeling refreshed as I dry off and wrap up in my robe.

I slip into bed and fire up my Mac scowling at the numerous emails still concerned about the number of exam rooms in the medical building. I respond to each of them in turn as most of them have not copied each other on them, but have copied their department teams as well as the Core Team comprised of Chase, Jenny, Terry, myself, the general contractor and a few representatives of the users on the team.

I reach Terry's note and see that he's probably gotten concerned with all the emails, to the point he felt it necessary to come up with some backup alternatives. I review Terry's email and smile at his willingness to go the extra mile.

TO: KMeilers@TorzialConsulting.org

From: TPartes@Martel&Sons.org
CC: CHPrestian@PrestianCorp.org,
JWarling@TorzialConsulting.org

KATE,

IT APPEARS Renee has set up everything needed for the simulation, but we are still getting moderate resistance to the exam rooms. I know you didn't want me to spend too much time creating alternative drawings, but I was able to put together a few quick models just in the event they are needed.

PLEASE LET me know if there is anything else you might need, before Monday. Otherwise, I look forward to seeing you and the demonstration.

Thanks,
Terry

TERRY PARTES
Lead Architect
Martel and Sons

TO: TPartes@Martel&Sons.org
From: KMeilers@TorzialConsulting.org
CC: CHPrestian@PrestianCorp.org,
JWarling@TorzialConsulting.org

HI TERRY,
Since you've created alternative designs with more exam rooms, I

would love to run them through the simulation on Monday, as long as you aren't opposed.

Please let me know.

THANKS,

Kate

Kate Meilers

Project Consultant

Torzial Consulting Firm.

TO: <u>KMeilers@TorzialConsulting.org</u>

From: <u>CHPrestian@PrestianCorp.org</u>

YOU HAVE ME INTRIGUED.... Why are you online?

C. **H. Prestian**

Chief Executive Officer, Owner

Prestian Corporation

TO: <u>CHPrestian@PrestianCorp.org</u>

From: <u>KMeilers@TorzialConsulting.org</u>

BECAUSE I HAVE work to do! What is intriguing?

KATE

Kate Meilers

Project Consultant

Torzial Consulting Firm

TO: KMeilers@TorzialConsulting.org
    From: CHPrestian@PrestianCorp.org

WHY SIMULATE options you don't want to design to?

C. **H. Prestian**
    Chief Executive Officer, Owner
    Prestian Corporation

TO: CHPrestian@PrestianCorp.org
    From: KMeilers@TorzialConsulting.org

YOU'LL SEE...
    Kate
    Kate Meilers
    Project Consultant
    Torzial Consulting Firm

TO: KMeilers@TorzialConsulting.org
    From: TPartes@Martel&Sons.org
    CC: CHPrestian@PrestianCorp.org,
    JWarling@TorzialConsulting.org

.   .   .

YOU ARE MORE than welcome to use the alternative options in your simulation. Please let me know if you would like them uploaded similarly to the others. I'm happy to do this in preparation for Monday.

Thanks,

Terry

TERRY PARTES
Lead Architect
Martel and Sons

TO: TPartes@Martel&Sons.org
From: KMeilers@TorzialConsulting.org
CC: CHPrestian@PrestianCorp.org,
JWarling@TorzialConsulting.org

HI TERRY,

If you could upload them to the simulation software, that would be a great help. Would you also send me the alternative options and the specs on each choice tonight?

Thanks,

Kate

Kate Meilers
Project Consultant
Torzial Consulting Firm

TO: KMeilers@TorzialConsulting.org
From: CHPrestian@PrestianCorp.org

. . .

WHY DO you care what the specs are on designs we shouldn't spend money on drawing and never intend to use?

C. H. Prestian
Chief Executive Officer, Owner
Prestian Corporation

TO: CHPrestian@PrestianCorp.org
From: KMeilers@TorzialConsulting.org

TRUST ME...

KATE

KATE MEILERS
Project Consultant
Torzial Consulting Firm

TO: KMeilers@TorzialConsulting.org
From: CHPrestian@PrestianCorp.org

BABY, I trust you completely. I'm just very curious and interested. How much longer are you going to work?

C. H. Prestian
Chief Executive Officer, Owner

Prestian Corporation

TO: <u>CHPrestian@PrestianCorp.org</u>
   From: <u>KMeilers@TorzialConsulting.org</u>

IF HE SENDS me the specs maybe an hour, shouldn't take much more than that. In the meantime, I think I'll pour another glass of this lovely wine and finish catching up on emails.
   Kate

KATE MEILERS
   Project Consultant
   Torzial Consulting Firm

TO: <u>KMeilers@TorzialConsulting.org</u>
   From: <u>CHPrestian@PrestianCorp.org</u>

DONE, Baby?
   C. H. Prestian
   Chief Executive Officer, Owner
   Prestian Corporation

TO: <u>CHPrestian@PrestianCorp.org</u>
   From: <u>KMeilers@TorzialConsulting.org</u>

. . .

ALMOST ... Come and share a glass of wine with me. I'm in the mood for a shower show.

KATE

KATE MEILERS
Project Consultant
Torzial Consulting Firm

TO: <u>KMeilers@TorzialConsulting.org</u>
    From: <u>CHPrestian@PrestianCorp.org</u>

BABY, you need only ask once.

C. **H. Prestian**
   Chief Executive Officer, Owner
   Prestian Corporation

YIKES... He's really on his way up. I remember the night in Aruba I invited him to my room and how disappointed I was when he didn't take me up on the offer. Now he's on his way up. I've never done this in front of someone before. I look at myself in the mirror and decide the nightgown will do. It's short, lacy and I feel sexy in it. The door opens, and the look in his eyes is all I need to see. He crosses the room in a few strides crushing me to him and capturing my lips with his.

"Baby, I've been waiting for you to invite me to watch you since the last time," he groans pressing my body into his. He takes the glass from my hand and offers me a sip. I feel it's warmth on the back of my throat and hope it gives me a little more confidence.

"Baby, I want to see this very much. Do you know how many times I've thought about this since that night?" he asks, taking my hand and guiding me to the bathroom.

He kisses me on the lips. "Finish your drink while I get the temperature adjusted," he instructs. I take another large sip of wine trying to calm my nerves. *Why am I so nervous?* He turns from the shower, and his eyes are smoldering.

"Baby, this time I don't want you to think about rubbing yourself because someone else can't please you. I want you to think about how sexy you are and how much you turn me on. Lift your arms for me, Baby," he instructs. I do, and he pulls my nightgown over my head rubbing my nipples gently, before urging me under the warmth of the shower. He strips out of his clothes, and his deep green eyes are absolutely smoldering with desire.

"Baby, show me what I missed in Aruba..." I feel myself moistening immediately. God, he is hot, and I wanted him the same way then that I want him now. He makes me feel so sexy when he talks to me like that. I back into the water letting it rain on me, feeling its warmth, knowing he's watching. I pour body wash into my hand, warming it and slowly rub it over my neck and arms allowing my fingers to find my nipples, squeezing, and rolling them in between each of my fingers so they elongate. At some point, I stop thinking, and my senses take over... the sudsy bubbles allow my fingers to glide smoothly over my heated skin, across my nipples, abdomen and navel and then lower.

I press myself against the back of the shower wall as my fingers make their way through the soft hair of my most intimate area, spreading myself for him. I relish in his audible gasp. "Baby, that's so hot...please don't stop," he moans. My fingers know exactly what feels good, and I rub slowly, at first, then faster as my need grows.

"Honey, take the showerhead down for me," I ask.

He reaches up and pulls the highest showerhead down, handing it to me. His eyes are filled with desire and lust. It is intoxicating to me.

"Rub your cock while you watch this."

"Baby..." he says, soaping himself and slowly rubbing his cock for me. I move the dial to pulse, and slowly run the water over my chest and then lower it across my abdomen. My fingers move apart, allowing him to view the water as it pulses over my clit. His cock is rock hard, and the look in his eyes is molten... his desire drives me over the edge and I can't control the orgasm that takes me as the water washes over me.

He turns me around pulling me back at the waist so I am bent over and thrusts inside of me, deep. I gasp at the depth and power of his urgency as he pushes me against the shower wall, taking me until he brings us both over the edge and we are quivering with abandoned need.

I wake, and Chase is already up and probably in the gym. I wrap my robe around me and go outside to call my mom. It's been three days since I met my dad. I can't put this off anymore, I need to find the nerve to tell her and see if she is interested in seeing him again. I hit her number and wait with bated breath as the phone dials.

"Hello," she says.

"Hi Mom," I say, uncertain of where to start.

"Hi, Sweetie," she says and fortunately, she takes over the conversation like only moms can do. We talk about the weather in Florida and Chicago, and the client she most recently signed.

I adopt a deep breath. "Mom, I need to speak with you, but I'm really not sure where to start. I know you didn't want me to pursue learning who my dad was or meeting him, but..."

"Katie, what do I have to do to make you realize the danger?" she admonishes.

"Mom, listen to me, please. I'm sorry, but I just couldn't get the thought that I have a father out of my mind. Chase told you his family is friends with Dad's family. Chase's dad, Don, talked to Carlos and explained the situation to Dad. He wanted to meet me, Mom, so I did.

"Oh, dear God," she says.

"Mom, I'm sorry. I know how concerned you are, but we met at Chase's dad's home in New York City. He was very nice and told me that he does not blame you for leaving. He blames himself and regrets not being upfront with you in the first place. He said in no uncertain circumstances that if he knew you were alive, nothing would have stopped him from finding you and that you are the only one he has ever loved. Mom, he wants to meet with you. He also mentioned that legally you are still his wife. Chase told me that he will work with him to develop a plan to make sure that none of his family or business associates pose a safety threat," I explain.

"Katie, I am glad that you were able to meet your dad, and that he had a chance to meet you, but it is not safe to make this public. If you do that, you and I will both be in danger. He knows this, Katie," she says. The fear in her voice is unmistakable, and I wonder for a moment if I've made a grave mistake.

"Mom, he and Chase are working on a plan to keep us safe," I say trying my best to reassure her, although now I am having second thoughts.

"Katie, you're as stubborn as he is. I should have never told you!"

"Mom, you know that's not true. I'm glad you shared it with me. We just have to work things out," I say, trying to reason with her.

"I have his personal phone number if you want it, Mom," I say.

"I'll think about it, Katarina," she says, ignoring my attempts to engage her in a walk down memory lane. We talk for a few more moments before I hang up and go in search of Chase. The dining room is empty, but his Mac and the newspaper are lying open on the table.

CHICAGO MIDWESTERN

Prestian Corporation files for national expansion
Nate Collins Freelance Journalist

THE PRESTIAN MEDICAL Facility has filed plans for state approval to embark on a multi- facility building project in the state of Illinois with two facilities in the inner city of Chicago and one in the southern part of the state. Plans for future expansions include national coverage in thirty-one states without union representation.

"Oh, shit, what the hell."

Message: Chase where are you?

Reply: In the gym, Baby.

Message: I saw the paper.
Reply: Be down in fifteen minutes.

I AM HAVING COFFEE, and Gaby has made omelets for breakfast when Chase gets finished working out. He pours himself a cup of coffee and sits down beside me at the kitchen table.

How did the press know about the expansions, Chase?" I ask.

"We are looking into it, but unfortunately, it appears the information was leaked by someone close to us," he says.

"I don't understand, Chase. How do you know that?"

"Baby, we still have a lot of work to do to confirm, but it would appear that one of your emails to Jenny was used as the platform for the story," he says.

"You don't think that Jenny had anything to do with it, Chase? She would never do anything like this."

"Katarina, it's not Jenny. She would have nothing to gain by having the national expansion placed in jeopardy. In fact, if we don't expand the model on a national level, she will lose the ability to triple her company and everything we just talked about last week. Someone who has access to her email leaked the story, and we're looking into who and why. Until we find out I don't want you to mention this to Jenny," he says.

"Chase, surely she's going to see the newspaper."

"I'm sure she will, but I don't want to tip our hand to whoever did this by having her act suspiciously. I just need a little time, Katarina."

"Okay, but I hate not being able to talk to Jenny about it. On a different note, I did talk to Mom this morning and told her that I met my dad," I say.

"Oh," he says eyebrows raised. "How did she take that?"

"Well, she wasn't exactly pleased if you can imagine her wrath, but I asked her to take his number."

"At least, that's something," he says.

"Jenny and I have been working on the structure proposal for the Prestian Corp division of Torzial on email," I say.

"Glad to hear it. I'm anxious to see it," he says.

"We have a little more work to do, and then we'll show you. In fact, we're meeting for lunch today to review it," I say.

I look down at the incoming message on my phone.

Message: Text me his phone number.

Chase is watching me, and his eyebrows rise in question. I smile. "Mom wants his phone number," I say.

"Indeed. I talked to Carlos yesterday, and he is anxious to speak with her, too," he says.

I look up in surprise. "What were you talking to him about?" I ask, curiosity getting the better of me.

"You, your mom, mostly future plans to ensure his family accepts you and your mom when the time is right. I invited him over Saturday evening for dinner," he says, gauging my reaction.

"He's coming to Chicago?" I say.

"He wanted to see you again, and I would prefer you not do that in New York until we have plans in place."

Chase is apparently taking control again. *Why does this surprise me?* I walk around the table and give him a kiss. "I love you very much and thank you for inviting him. I told Jenny I would meet her at Torzial. How long do you think before we can let Jenny know what's happening with the news story? She's my dearest friend, and I hate the fact that someone is intentionally trying to sabotage this project. It affects both of the companies."

"Not long, Baby. Just give me a bit," he says, kissing me soundly on the lips. "I'll let Jay know that we're heading into the city in a couple hours. Now go and get your shower before I decide we should cancel the work day and spend it in bed."

JAY DROPS me off at Torzial and by the end of the day, Jenny and I have finished the structural proposal for the Prestian Corp division of Torzial, the positions, job descriptions, and organizational reporting structure. "I'll send Chase a note and find out when he wants to meet and go over the proposal. I think we've got a solid plan," she says.

Chase is in his office when I get back to Prestian Corp, and someone is talking on the speakerphone. He waves for me to come in and close the door. "We've reached out to the state to find out why the plans are not back yet, but haven't received any response. I contacted an old colleague of mine that works on the approval committee, and while he couldn't say much, he did confirm plans are being held up due to the union unrest. Whoever leaked the national expansion project knew it was worth millions of dollars the unions would want or else they're working for the unions. Any word on who yet, Chase?" the voice on the speakerphone says.

"Yes, we just found out this morning, Brian. I need to talk to Katarina before we proceed, but I'll get back to you later this afternoon," he says before disconnecting.

"You found out who leaked the expansion information to the unions?" I ask hesitantly.

"We did. Katarina, it was Ty... Jenny's boyfriend," he says.

"Chase, that can't be right. Why in the world would he want to do that to Jenny and to us for that matter?" I say, trying to make sense of the situation.

"Katarina there are millions of dollars of opportunity in operations such as these. The unions want their share, and he knows it, but that's just the tip of the iceberg. The information he leaked about the drug costs being combined into part of the patient cost and not a separate fee was not unintentional. The pharmaceutical companies make billions of dollars in profit each year on each medication they sell, and you can be sure they have a few politicians in their back pocket. Ty is a shrewd attorney, and he makes millions by watching out for the larger corporations. We're going to need to meet with him and Jenny," he says.

"Chase, she is going to be devastated when she finds out. She actually cares a great deal about him," I say.

"I know, Baby. There's really no easy way to do this, but she needs to be in the room when I confront, Ty."

"Were you able to complete the structural proposal?" he asks.

"We did, in fact, she was going to send you a note later in the day to see if you wanted to meet and review it."

"Good, then I'll schedule a meeting and include Ty since he's the attorney that participated in the last agreement. In the meantime... I know it's going to be hard for you not to say anything, but I'm trusting that you won't," he says.

"I won't say a word, but it makes my blood boil just thinking about it," I say.

I'm going to send Jenny a note to see if they can meet with us this week. I need a couple days to gather more information and mitigate the damage he's done," he says.

Jenny and Ty are already in her office when Chase and I arrive. Jay and his crew are posted outside the suites. Chase pulls out a chair for me and greets Jenny and Ty. "Jenny it's good to see you. Ty, thanks for taking the time to come. Jenny sent me a draft of the structural proposal for the Torzial Division that will be focused on the Prestian Medical Facilities. I think it looks like a sound business plan, and I would like to proceed. I've drafted a contract that includes the terms and conditions that she and I spoke of previously," he says, handing a document to Ty.

"I have to say I'm a little surprised that you're moving so quickly. I've been following the newspaper and the unions don't seem to be backing down on the pressure now that they know it's not just a couple of facilities in Chicago they're losing out on," he says.

"I think after today the unions will have nothing to worry about, Ty. You see I met with the union leaders this morning, and they were led to believe that none of the Prestian Corporation facilities would be using union labor. It was easy to set the record straight after I read the email that you sent to them," he says.

"I don't think I understand what you mean, Chase."

"On the contrary, I believe that you know exactly what I am talking about, Ty. The letter that you emailed Frank Cohen last month divulged details of an expansion that only myself, Brian my COO, Katarina and Jenny knew about. You used information obtained from Jenny's computer to create a burning platform for the unions that did not exist. You traded information to profit knowing it would mean drawing a halt to all future expansions and that the success of Jenny's company was riding on it. You knew that and still you sold out. The five million dollars transferred to your account was easy to trace, Ty. It wasn't as easy to deal with the pharmaceutical companies. We are still in conversations about creating a package that will ensure all patients receive medicine they need, and that pharmaceutical companies continue to be well compensated for putting that money back into further research. To date, you have been given a five million dollar check from each of the three largest pharmaceutical companies in the world, based on false information. I believe they would like this money back and can be quite persuasive," Chase says.

"Jenny I am sorry you had to hear it this way. I needed to meet with the unions this morning before I knew that we could move forward with the facility expansion. Feel free to review the contract and contact me in the next week or so. Please do understand, however, that I will ask that you retain a different attorney and have made a note of this in one of the clauses," he says, pulling my chair out for me and guiding me out of the room. Jay, Matt, and Sheldon follow us into the elevator. Jay takes the earbud out of his ear, and Chase reaches into his suit pocket and hands Jay a small recorder. "Just in case Ty got out of control," Jay assures me, seeing my look of surprise. "It's not every day you get told that you just lost twenty million dollars," he says.

"I need to call Jenny," I say to Chase. "Did you see the look on her face? She seemed to play it off kind of cool, but she must be hurting to know he would sell her and the company she loves so much out like that," I say.

"Give her some time, Baby. Ty will probably try to fill her head with a lot of bullshit. She'll need a friend to help sort through it all."

I'm clearing dinner when I get a text from Jenny.

Message: Have time to come over? Ty's gone.

Reply: Of course.

Message: Thanks.

"Chase, I'm going to Jenny's. I'm not sure what's going on, but she wants me to come over. She said Ty's not there," I say, seeing the flash of unease cross his features.

"Let me get hold of Jay and make sure they have security in place in the event he goes to see her," he says.

"Thanks, Honey," I say, leaning over to kiss him.

"Of course," he says. Matt and Sheldon are already in the car when the driver draws up to the entrance to collect me. Jay must have given them the address since he already knows where he's going. The driver pulls over to the curb a block from her house, and Matt and Sheldon get out.

"Kate, we'll be right outside," he says before the driver continues to Jenny's home.

I walk up to her door and knock. She answers it in her robe with wet hair, and I gasp as she looks up at me. Her lip is split open, and I can tell she's been crying.

"Jenny, what the hell happened?" I ask, closing the door and giving her a big hug.

"He didn't deny anything. He said that he has to look out for the big industries because they pay his salary and it was nothing personal. I told him that he knew that if Chase didn't expand nationally that I would not have the business to expand. I said it's nothing personal my ass, and he slapped me," she says, tears filling her eyes.

"Jenny, that is assault, you should report it," I say fuming.

"Just leave it, Kate. It's just over. On our way home tonight he had a couple calls from the pharmaceutical companies. At least, I think that's who they were. Chase was right, they want all their money back, and they want it now. He was in a foul temper, and I personally think he may be in way over his head," she says.

I open a bottle of wine and pour a glass for each of us. Jenny is seated on the couch, and as I bend down to hand her a drink she reaches up, and the sleeve of her robe slides down her arm revealing a large red burn mark.

"Jenny, what the hell is this?" I ask, putting my glass down. I push the sleeve of her other arm up, and the same mark exists. I suddenly feel sick to my stomach at the realization. She has been tied up roughly. She is just looking at me blankly and shakes her head as the tears continue to fall. "Jenny, talk to me. What happened," I urge gently, sitting down beside her to take her in my arms and comfort her.

"He slapped me, tied me up... and then he raped me," she stammers. She is sobbing uncontrollably now, and I hold her close. "I tried and tried, but I couldn't get free, and I couldn't push him off of me. He turned into someone different tonight. He wanted to hurt me and was laughing," she says between sobs.

I rock her as she continues to cry. "Jenny, you have to turn this in. He can't rape you and get away with this," I say seething with anger.

"He can get away with it, Kate. I threatened to call the police, and he just laughed and slapped me again. He said if I went to the police that he would have the books for Torzial opened for investigation."

She is rambling. "Jenny, slow down. Breathe deeply and tell me what he said," I say.

"He has been using Torzial accounts to launder money and who knows what else. The entire company will fold if he divulges this, and he will if I turn him in," she says.

I hold my dearest friend close and just listen for a while. "Jenny, even if you don't think you can turn him in, I believe that you need to go to the hospital and get an exam. Get the burns on your arms documented; get an examination for the record. You said he was rough with you, are you okay down there, torn or anything?" I ask, gently probing.

"I'm not going, Kate. I just needed someone to talk to."

"Okay, the last question then. Are you protected from pregnancy?" I ask.

"I've been on the pill for years."

We spend the better part of the night talking, and she drinks more than I have ever seen her drink, ever. My efforts to encourage her to slow down are met with a serious scowl. I stay with her until she succumbs to exhaustion and the effects of too many glasses of wine, before tucking her in on the couch with a quilt and a pillow from her room.

MESSAGE: Can you have security stay at Jenny's? I'll leave when they take over.

Reply: Yes, what's wrong?

Message: Please make sure Ty doesn't get close to her. We can talk when I get home.

Reply: Jay is on his way to pick you up. Matt and Sheldon will stay.

When I get home, Chase is lounging in bed working on his laptop. I undress and don't bother with a nightgown, crawling into bed beside him.

He puts the laptop to the side and pulls me into his arms. "What is it, Baby?" he says, pushing my hair out of my face so he can see my eyes.

The dam bursts and I can't control the flood of tears that I've been holding back all night.

His eyes are wild with concern, and he takes my face in his hands. "Katarina, tell me what is wrong," he demands.

"When Jenny and Ty left the pharmaceutical companies called him, and they want their money back. She confronted him about what he did, and he just said it was his job to take care of the big businesses. She said he was in a nasty mood, but he's never been violent before." His eyes harden and his jaw tenses.

"What happened, Katarina?" he asks.

"Ty snapped tonight. He hit Jenny and tied her up, and he... he raped her, Chase. She's got rope burns all over her arms. She said he meant to hurt her, and she must have struggled a lot." I am sobbing now, and his face is livid.

"I couldn't get her to go to the hospital, and she can't go to the police because Ty has been using her company to launder money and will expose it, indicting her for it, if she does," I explain, wiping my tears.

"Fuck," he says, getting out of bed and pulling his jeans on over his nakedness.

"Where are you going?" I ask.

"To make this right," he says, and I've seen the look in his eyes before.

"Chase, at least, tell me what you are going to do. I promised Jenny I would keep this in confidence," I say.

"Katarina, she did not deserve what he did to her, and I'll be damned if she lives with the threat of someone blackmailing her for the rest of her life," he says.

He pushes a button on his phone before he walks onto the balcony. "Jay, this is Chase," is all I hear before the balcony door slides shut.

Shit, shit, shit... What the hell is he doing?

When he comes back in, he is calmer, but his eyes are hooded, and he gives nothing away. He unbuttons his jeans, and I can't help admire his body as he slides into bed with me.

"Talk to me, Chase," I say.

"What do you want me to tell you?"

"Anything… just say something. Tell me what you are doing," I plead.

"Katarina, you're not going to like it, so why have me share this with you?"

"I might not like it, but I need to know, Chase."

"I am having someone confiscate all his files, electronic and paper, from his office. Once we have those he will no longer be in a position to threaten Jenny. My guess is he has a lot of information to hide and is being paid quite well to launder it and bury the evidence. He was rash tonight and will be trying to cover his tracks come tomorrow. We'll need to work on finding the compromised accounts and create a different money trail. Look at me, Baby. If we don't do this, Jenny will be at his mercy for the rest of her life. Do you understand what that means? Anytime he decides he wants to rape her again, he can. He will have power over her," he says.

"I never thought about it in that way, and I don't believe she did either," I say, lying next to him with my head on his chest. My heart constricts with the love I feel for him and the way he takes care of the people we care about. My phone beeps again reminding me of a missed message. I reach over to check the call and hit the button to play the message. Mom has talked to my dad, and I don't think I imagine the excitement in her voice. Her message lets me know that she and Chase have spoken and that he is flying her to Chicago to see my dad for the first time in twenty-six years. There is so much running through my mind.

"The message was from my mom. You're flying her here, tomorrow, to meet my dad?" I ask, puzzled.

"I am. She couldn't reach you on your cell so she called me. She wants to meet your dad, and I told her he would be having dinner with us tomorrow and invited her to join us. She was going to book a flight, and I offered the plane," he says as if it was the most logical thing in the world. We'll head back home early tomorrow and can work from there until your mom arrives.

"So are you done working tonight?" I ask.

"I am except for a few calls later on. But for now, all the arrangements are made. Your mom should be landing around noon, and your dad will be here for dinner," he says.

I pull him closer to my body, needing to hold him close and capture his lips with my own. He embraces me and holds me tighter.

"Tonight, though, I have you all to myself, Baby," he says.

ELEVEN

The vista of pink and blue hues glowing around the rising sun is stunning as we lift off over the lake and toward the country house. "I need to patch into a call from my study but I won't be too long," Chase says as we land and walk toward the house.

"That's okay. I need to call Jenny and see how she's doing. I didn't want to call too early," I say.

"Speaking of," Chase says, glancing down at his phone. "Text from Matt. She's up and moving around."

"I'm pretty sure she must have a terrible headache after all the wine she drank last night. I think I'll give her a little time to eat and get a run in before I call," I say.

"Did you let the security team know?" Chase asks.

"What, they didn't alert you?" I counter, feigning my sweetest smile.

"Careful Baby, I could cancel my meeting just as easy and it would be a much more pleasurable morning," he says.

"I'll take a rain check," I say, kissing him on the lips before heading upstairs to change.

Chase is at the table when I return from my run. He has his laptop and coffee in front of him and looks grim. "What's the matter?" I ask, seeing the consternation on his face.

"Baby, sit down, we need to talk," he says, pouring a cup of coffee from the carafe into the cup in front of me.

"Your mother did not make the plane trip," he says. He is watchful, pensive almost, taking in my response.

"Did she change her mind?" I ask, fearful as I note the twitching of his jaw and darkness in his eyes.

"Baby, I wish I could tell you, but we don't know yet. We sent a driver to pick her up and take her to the airport, and she didn't answer the door. She put an end to the round the clock security early last week saying she wanted her privacy back. The driver called in for backup and when they went in her suitcase was half packed and lying on the floor. They found a travel bag filled with makeup left open in the bathroom, suggesting that she planned to make the trip today. Her car is still in the garage, and there were no signs of forced entry or scuffle in the home, Katarina. We are tracking her email accounts and phone records and are contacting all the cab and shuttle companies in the area, Baby," he says.

"Oh, my God. My mom's worst nightmare is coming true. She was petrified that once someone learned of our existence, they would come after her. This is my fault," I say, registering the gravity of the situation.

"Baby, don't. I know what's running through your head. I have a call into Carlos, and he's already on his way from New York. He told me he has not spoken to anyone about you or your mom, but he has been on the phone with her for hours since you gave her his number. It's possible that someone could have had his phone tapped and learned about her that way, Katarina. It's also a very real possibility that she ran, again. Carlos said they argued last night when they talked about announcing you both to the family," he says.

"Chase, she would not leave me. Something bad has happened to my mother," I say, dismissing the possibility immediately.

"We'll get to the bottom of it, Katarina. In the meantime, get something to eat while I make a few phone calls. Your dad will be here shortly. I had the jet flown in for him in case someone is monitoring his corporate flight plans," he says.

"Did you call the police?" I ask, although in my heart I already know the answer.

"Katarina, we'll report it once I know a little more. Right now our team is in the house sweeping for fingerprints and taps," he says. His eyes are dark, probing and gauging my reaction.

I silently will myself to appear calm, but my heart is racing. If I had listened to my mom, she'd still be here. Why in the world would she have taps in her house?

Chase folds me into his arms. "Baby, you're trembling. We will find her," he says trying to comfort me, but the dam suddenly bursts, and I am inconsolable. The tears flood down my face and I can't stop shaking. He lifts me into his arms and carries me into our bedroom and lays down beside me. "Baby, we are going to find her," he says, rocking me as he pulls me close to his body and draws the comforter over the top of us. Even fully clothed I am frozen and unable to control my trembling.

"I love you, more than anything, Baby," he whispers, and that's the last thing I hear as I fall into a deeply troubled sleep.

When I wake he is still lying next to me but is working on his Mac and his phone is by his side.

"Any word?" I ask quietly.

"Not yet Baby," he says, pushing the hair out of my eyes and leaning down to kiss me. "Your dad landed a short while ago and is on his way here with Jay," he says.

The housekeeper announces Carlos and his eyes capture mine the minute my dad walks through the door. "Chase, it's good to see you and I appreciate you sending the jet," he says to Chase, but his eyes never leave mine. "Katarina, I want you to know I told absolutely no one about your mother, but if someone was tapped in, it's a possibility they could have learned of her existence. We will find her, Katarina," he says, his eyes filled with resolve.

"Carlos, I'm glad you could make it, and I understand how much Karissa and now Katarina must mean to you, but I need to be sure that your family was not involved in the disappearance of Katarina's mother," Chase says.

"Chase, I know where you are going with this. I've already contacted the family. We are meeting in New York tomorrow evening which will allow my nephews time to fly back into the country. They are leaving this afternoon," he says.

My face must show my confusion. "Katarina, when a family meeting is called by the head of the family, everyone is in attendance. I would like for you and Chase to be there, as well," he says.

Chase answers an incoming call, but his eyes don't leave mine. "No, I want all the airlines, bus stations, and car rentals checked. We can't rule out the fact that she might have gotten scared and run. No, she's too smart for that, Jay. She's managed to keep her identity hidden for years. Keep me posted," he says disconnecting.

Chase and my dad spend the next several hours going over the conversations he and my mother have had during the previous week. "All of the calls have been amiable, and your mom agreed to meet with me two days ago. We've talked since and she seemed to be looking forward to it as much as I was." Chase presses him for details of their conversation. He explains the conversation the previous night with trepidation. "We did not fight, but she is still very much afraid of the family's lifestyle and did not want me to tell them about her or you. I explained that I am now the head of the household, and they will respect my wishes," he says, but needed more time to think about it. Before Karissa hung up she told me that she would see me today," he says.

Chase and Carlos are busy taking calls from Jay, who has security running an investigation on all of the transportation options in and out of the city, checking her credit card against recent purchases, and another team working on her cell and email activity.

I head toward our bedroom and hit the button to connect to Jenny as I close the door behind me. "How are you doing, Jenny?" I ask as she picks up.

"Still a little hungover, but I'll survive. Thanks for coming over last night," she says.

"Where else would I be? Did you consider going to the hospital anymore?" I ask.

"No, it's done, Kate. I just want to forget it ever happened."

I decide not to push, and we spend a few more moments on the phone before she disconnects to take some more ibuprofen and rest. I sign onto work email going through each and responding as needed. There is discord among the designers about the placement of the facility on the land, but overall the contract negotiations are going well, and it appears we are ahead of schedule. The swoosh of my phone alerts me to an incoming text.

Message: You awake, Baby?

Reply: Yes, just working on the facility placement.

Message: I saw the emails. What exactly are you doing?

Reply: Developing decision-making criteria. Why?

Message: Just interested in how this debate will play out.

Reply: We are going to let the patient's needs and best interests settle it!

Message: That's my girl! Don't stay up too late. It'll be awhile before we are finished.

Reply: No news?

Message: Not yet. Soon.

IT TAKES a couple hours to compile the data for the decision-making tool and when it's complete I send it off to the designers copying Jenny, Chase and Brian, his Chief Operating Officer. I finish brushing my teeth in the bathroom and walk into the bedroom, slowly discarding my clothes and climb into bed feeling tired and emotionally exhausted. I have almost fallen asleep when Chase returns to our room. My eyes are heavy with exhaustion, but I have a difficult time averting them from his stark-naked hardness and feel myself moistening at the sight of him. He slides into bed beside me and pulls me into his arms, pressing me against him, holding me close and protected. "Sleep, Baby," he says, rubbing my back as I drift off to sleep to the sound of his heartbeat.

The helicopter is waiting to take the security team and all three of us to the airport in the morning. When we land at O'Hare, there is a flurry of activity on the tarmac. Jay and his crew get out of the helicopter first, and appear to be talking with the other men who are moving between cars and the waiting jet.

"Chase, I just saw Matt get on the airplane," I say, looking out the window.

"Yes, Jay has another team keeping an eye on Jenny and taking care of things on that front. He and Sheldon are coming with us," he says.

"Chase, one of our men is new to the team. Jay isn't allowing him on the plane," Carlos says.

"Then he goes commercial. Jay has full command of the security teams," Chase says, his eyes hooded and controlled.

"Have him meet us back at the house and next time make damn sure he's included on the list you provide to Jay," Carlos says into the phone.

THE FLIGHT to New York is quick and uneventful. Carlos has his limo driver waiting, and he greets us as we walk down the ramp. Jay and his team get into a car that stays behind us as we head into the heavy morning traffic. The driver navigates through the congestion for the next forty minutes until we turn off the main roads. The countryside is beautiful, and the leaves are all starting to turn yellows, vibrant oranges and variations of red as we drive for another half an hour farther out of the city. I'm not at all surprised when we come to a massive stone and wrought iron gate before being allowed entry onto the property. I've seen this type of security at Chase's. The driver continues once the gates lift for what seems another mile before the home comes into view. It looks like a three story Victorian mansion. There is, at least, a ten bay parking garage attached to the home. The driver follows the long circular drive and pulls up to the entrance. Carlos takes my hand to assist me out of the back seat. Jay and Chase are conferring quietly, and I wonder what, if anything, Jay has learned.

We are escorted into a sprawling foyer with a black and white marble floor. The decor extends to the curved staircase which winds along the side of the room. We follow Carlos through a vast living area where he gestures for us to take a seat. The living room has a black grand piano in the corner, and the windows overlook a spacious lawn and woods. The fireplace appears to be made of black marble, and I almost gasp when I see the portraits hung over its mantle. The painting in the middle is my mom and Carlos on their wedding day. Her auburn hair is long, hanging past her shoulders and her white gown is flowing around her on a green lawn. Carlos is smiling and dressed in a black tuxedo. The pictures on either side of it are of my mother. She is laughing and smiling in both, and it causes a lump in my throat as I try hard not to think about what might have happened to her. "Come, please make yourselves at home," he says, pouring a glass of wine for each of us at the marble bar. "The formal dining room is being set up as we speak. Members of our family should be arriving shortly."

"Katarina, I want you to be prepared for what it is that I intend with this meeting. Chase and I have discussed this at length, but I don't want you to be caught off guard. I am going to introduce you as my daughter. I expect that you will be welcomed with open arms by my family. Everyone will know you are my daughter as soon as they see you since the likeness to your mother is uncanny. I need to inform them that your mom is alive. It's the only way I can be sure that no one from our family has had involvement in her disappearance and gain their support and assistance in getting her back alive," he says. He is watchful, gauging my reaction.

"But, she didn't want you to tell them," I say, knowing in my heart that it has to be done.

"Katarina, it's the only way," Chase interjects, taking me by the hand for reassurance.

"Why don't we get situated and visit until everyone arrives. Bring your wine with you," Carlos says, guiding us through the living area into another spacious sitting area and then into what has to be the largest dining room I have ever seen. I look up and down the expanse of the sleek, shiny black table with enough chairs to seat twenty guests. Chase and I follow him to the head of the table, and he gestures to the chair on his right for me and waves Chase to take the seat next to that. Carlos greets each member of the family as they arrive, shaking hands with them one by one. When everyone is situated, he sits at the end of the table and only then does everyone else take their seat. He fastens a small device and clips it to his collar, and likewise, everyone in the room does the same thing. I look down and notice that Chase and I do not have what appear to be microphones.

"I appreciate everyone's attendance this evening. I know a few of you were out of the country, and it means a great deal to me that you traveled back to be with the family tonight. As you may have noticed, we have guests this evening. Chase Prestian is the son of Don Prestian, who you all know is a dear and close friend of mine. And this lovely lady is Katarina and more importantly, she is my daughter," he says, and his eyes are full of pride.

There are audible muffled gasps, and I feel embarrassed at the eyes turned my way.

"As most of you know, my wife Karissa, Katarina's mother, disappeared twenty-six years ago. Many of you were by my side, helping to search for her and were there to comfort me when at last the effort seemed futile. I will never forget that kindness. Karissa left because I was dishonest with her, leading her to believe she was marrying a fine upstanding businessman. Upon discovering the truth, and terrified, she fled this way of life and soon learned of her pregnancy. She feared returning would put her and her unborn child in danger.

"She worried, and still fears she will not be welcomed back. Her concern gravely distresses me. She and I have recently had many conversations about this, and I have assured her that as my wife, she will be welcomed with open arms by anyone in my family. It is clear there was never any intent to harm the family as she has kept her knowledge of the family business safeguarded all of these years. Please speak now if anyone at the table is unable to fully support this," he says, scanning the length of the table... completely in control. "Now, I need to know if anyone here already knew about my wife and daughter?" he asks again, looking at each face down the expanse of the table. "My wife was deathly afraid that she or Katarina would be in harm's way if her identity were learned. I convinced her to come out of hiding and meet with me; however, she disappeared before the meeting could occur. We are investigating every lead thus far, but I need to make sure that no one in this family was in any way, shape or form involved with Karissa's disappearance." There is shaking of heads all the way down the table signaling no involvement from any of the family. "Good, then I need to ask everyone to assist us as we work to find her. Lastly, if you would be so kind to take turns introducing yourselves to my daughter I would greatly appreciate it," he says.

They are in the process of sharing their names and where they live when Chase looks down at his vibrating phone, which is on silent. He stands abruptly to take the call and taps Carlos on the shoulder. "It's Karissa's number," he says, answering the phone immediately.

"Karissa," Chase says, listening intently to the voice on the other line. "I'll be waiting," he says after a short while.

"Chase what happened?" I ask, and everyone has stopped and is openly staring at us.

"Do you want me to discuss this here?" Chase asks Carlos.

"Yes, my family was not involved in her disappearance. I have their word," Carlos says, handing Chase a small microphone.

"The call I answered was Karissa's phone. Otherwise, I would never have shown such disrespect," he explains to the members of the family. "The caller told me Karissa would be held hostage until enough merchandise was moved through United States customs to make up for the shipment which was lost last year. I can only assume the delivery being referred to is a drug shipment that was confiscated by Interpol last year. I was in the middle of a deal with Prince Alfreita in Saudi Arabia, and he invited me to meet him on his ship. We had a meal, concluded our business and I flew back to Saudi. Shortly after that, his boat was taken over by Interpol and a lot of drugs were found in the hull. He believes I leaked information to the authorities, and this must be his way of exacting retribution," he says, looking into my eyes.

"Did they give you any indication of when they would call back?" Carlos asks.

"No, the man on the other end of the line said that he would phone again with instructions," Chase says.

The heavyset man with graying hair at the end of the table speaks. He has a very deep and distinct voice, and his eyes are dark and wary. "We have intel on that operation," he says to Carlos.

"Chase and Katarina, if you will excuse us, I need to speak with the family. Maria will show you into the sitting room until I'm done," he says, as a woman with long hair pulled into a ponytail appears to escort us into the great room.

Chase pulls me into his lap on the couch and rubs the back of my neck. "Baby, I am so sorry. We'll get her back, Katarina. We're a step ahead now, we know who we are dealing with. I'm going to need to talk to Carlos when he gets done. There are going to be things about this mission that you may not want to know anything about, Baby," he says.

"Do whatever it takes to get my mom back, Chase. I promise I won't think any less of you or Carlos," I say, resting against his chest.

"We'll get her back, Baby," he says, wiping at the steady stream of tears falling onto my cheeks and his shirt.

Carlos joins us shortly, and I move off of Chase's lap, suddenly self-conscious under my father's scrutiny. "Chase, we need to talk," he says.

"I've told Katarina that we may be discussing things that are difficult for her to hear or comprehend, but that are necessary for getting her mom returned. She'd like to stay, Carlos. She understands the stakes here."

Carlos looks at me for affirmation, and I nod.

"Chase, what we're about to discuss stays in the room. I have your word?"

"You do, Carlos. What's on your mind?" Chase says, seeming entirely at ease with my father and not the least bit intimidated.

"Members of my family are responsible for tipping the authorities off to Prince Alfreita's shipment. I was not aware until this evening. The product was intended to undercut sales in the families' markets. Prince Alfreita and his business associates have been blatant about trying to impair the family business and have now taken my wife hostage.

"Carlos, you realize that he does not know she is your wife. He thinks he is getting back at me by holding my girlfriend's mom hostage until payment for his loss is collected," Chase says.

"I do realize that Chase, but it doesn't make a damn bit of difference to me. He has systematically been trying to drive my family out of the overseas territory for quite some time and now the bastard's got Karissa. He's passed the line of no return, Chase."

"I understand your feelings, Carlos. We'll get her back," Chase says.

"My understanding is that your security detail and intel capabilities far surpass those of our own and even the military. I'm not quite sure how you've pulled that off, but we could sure use ears on the ground, Chase."

"You can be assured intel, and anything else you need is at your disposal. I've already sent word to Jay. He's tracking the call from Karissa's phone, but my guess is that it may have been too short to learn anything substantial," Chase says.

TWELVE

We join the rest of the relatives and finish dinner, and it is late by the time the men finish talking and the family, one by one, stop to chat and welcome me. "Are you sure you won't stay the night?" Carlos asks.

"No, thanks for the offer, Carlos, but I'm afraid we need to get back to Chicago. I'll contact you as soon as I've had a chance to confer with Jay tonight," Chase says.

"I'll be waiting for your call. In the meantime, I've arranged for my helicopter to pick you up and take you back to the airport."

"Thank you, Carlos. Jay mentioned that you had arranged transport and he's got the security crew on standby at the airport," Chase says.

As soon as we board the jet and can freely move around the plane, I go into the bedroom, change into a pair of yoga pants and a sweat-shirt, and curl up on the bed. The evening has been an emotional introduction to my father's world. I'm still thinking about that when Chase comes in.

"How are you feeling, Katarina?" he asks.

"I've been better. Nothing like getting an up close and personal introduction to your father's world. I'm just trying to process it all," I say.

He kisses me gently. "Get some sleep, Katarina. I have some work to do in preparation for a meeting tomorrow, and I need to talk to Jay. I'll wake you before we land," he says.

"I'm not really tired. I think I'll work for a while and get my mind on something else," I say, leaning over to grab my Mac from the nightstand.

"Okay, Baby. This will be over soon," he says before closing the door.

I find myself reading the same email over and over and after a while close the computer cover. Chase and Jay are in the living area of the plane reviewing something on the laptop at the table by the window.

"Anything interesting?" I say, settling onto the couch and curling my legs underneath me.

"Just finalizing plans for the communications team. Are you cold, Baby?" Chase asks as I cover myself with the afghan that rests on the back of the sofa.

"Maybe just a little," I say.

"Let's get the fire going," Chase says, walking over to the floor-to-ceiling fireplace and starting it with the remote. The artificial fire ignites and almost immediately begins radiating warmth throughout the cabin. He walks over to the granite bar on the other side of the room and brings me a warm cup of coffee.

"Drink this," he says.

"It smells heavenly," I say, inhaling the sweet aroma. "What is it?"

"A little Baileys in a decaffeinated Brazilian coffee. It will relax you," he says.

"Thank you. It's wonderful," I say, taking a sip.

"You're welcome," he says, pouring two cups of coffee for himself and Jay before returning to his spot at the table.

"Thanks, Chase," Jay says, absently looking up. "I think we've got just about everything covered. The crews have all been notified. Some are already in flight and will arrive tonight and others first thing in the morning. All the communications have been routed, and we should be set."

"Great. I already let Gaby know we'll have a house full after tonight and will give Carlos a call once we land with an update," he says.

The next day is a blur. Chase and Jay have moved six people and a lot of equipment into a large common area in the back of the house. The room is full of computer monitors, headphones, overhead TV monitors, and speakers. More security teams arrive throughout the morning and are escorted to the lower level of the home. Gaby has a kitchen full of help who are busy cooking and making sure all the men have fresh coffee and enough to eat while we wait.

I head to the library, turn on the fireplace and snuggle into the oversized reading chair before I call Jenny. "Hi there," she says, answering on the first ring.

"Hi there, yourself. You sound a little better," I say.

"Yeah, a few gallons of water, ibuprofen, and sleep worked wonders," she says.

"I'm glad you feel better," I say.

"I was just reviewing the information you sent to the designers with the sunlight, distance to the parking lot, and other factors. I would love to be a fly on the wall when they start reading through it," she says laughing.

It is nice to hear her laugh. "I have to admit I was thinking the same thing myself. I might stay out of their way for a couple days," I say.

"I'll be interested in how they decide to lay the building as a result. Hey, I need to go, for now. I have to take another call," Jenny says.

"No problem, I'll talk to you tomorrow," I say before disconnecting.

CHASE and I are eating lunch in the kitchen when the phone rings. "It's your mom's phone," he says answering it. "Chase here," he says. "I am going to need confirmation that Karissa is still alive and unharmed. No, I want to talk to her. I am putting the lives of my men and my reputation on the line for a woman I barely know. You tell the prince that I want confirmation she is alive and unharmed, or the deal is off. Otherwise, I'll let her daughter know that I did everything I could, but it just wasn't enough," he says. He disconnects and captures my eyes with his. "Baby, I am so sorry you had to hear that, but I need them to think that I don't care about her. It's the only way to keep her safe.

They need these loads to get through customs, or the prince himself will be sought after by the men that have already received payment for this merchandise and can't deliver. His shipments have kept getting cut off, and he doesn't know how. Alfrieta needs an alternative way to get the product into the country which is why they are working with me. He's also got to be worried about the mafia, namely your family, coming after him when they learn he is trying to take over their market. He is unaware your father and family already know about him."

I HAVE LOST MY APPETITE, and instead of eating, sip on the lemon water in front of me. The minutes on the clock seem to pass by like hours. The beep on Chase's phone finally alerts us to the incoming call. He signals to Jay that it's her number and answers the call.

"Hello, Karissa this is Chase. We only have a few moments. Are you being fed and do you have enough water? Have any of these men assaulted you in any way?" he asks.

He probes her with a few more questions and then is silent. "I see, I will tell your daughter that you are fine. Can you put them back on the phone, please?" he asks, squeezing his eyes shut, resting his forehead on his hand.

"This is Chase. Your team seems to have kept their hands to themselves, and she is unharmed. Make sure she continues to get three meals a day, plenty of water and keep your hands off her. I want a scheduled call tomorrow. If it stays that way, I will make sure your product reaches its intended recipients. If instead, you fuck up my pussy supply by hurting her mom, I will let the mob know you are trying to take them out of the picture." He disconnects and I can't listen to anymore. I just need to move. I head to our bedroom and change into running gear. As I come down the stairs, he's walking up the stairs and captures my eyes with his.

"Don't Chase. I know you didn't mean it, but I just need to get the hell out of here for a while. Jay can follow me or not, but I need to go for a run," I say, passing him on the stairs and heading for the patio that will lead me to the path by the lake. I put in my earbuds and hit shuffle, allowing the music to eventually calm my nerves. My half-way song comes on, and I am not near ready to turn back. I continue along the lake path enthralled by the apple orchard that I haven't seen before and then a two story cabin comes into view. It's all knotty pine looking with a green roof, and there are about ten canoes and paddle boats on racks by the lake. This must be the boys and girls cabin that Gaby and Chase were talking about. I turn back and see Sheldon in the bushes ahead of me. I smile to myself. Security trying to stay clear of my line of site is funny.

I head into the house and am taken aback by the barrage of guests that have arrived. Don, Chase's dad, is sitting in the chair across from my father and members of the family I just met last night are seated in the living room. Our security team is in the room, minus the ones that were apparently traipsing after me. I feel fortunate I put on a t-shirt over my sports bra before I left. Chase stands when I walk into the room, and every man in attendance does likewise. I recognize some of them as my uncles and cousins, but many do not look familiar. *What the fuck...*

"Katarina, you met the men working on intel this morning. They have set up in one of the back offices and will be keeping tabs on cell phone activity, ship radio communications and land to air communications. The team you see before you will be working on the plan to extract your mom once we locate her through that intel," he says by way of introduction.

Three servers are walking around the room with trays of bars and flavored regular and decaffeinated coffees. Gaby is doing whatever she can to make the guests and the situation less stressful for all involved. That puts me into gear. I quickly run upstairs to shower, get redressed and head into the kitchen to find Gaby. These people are in our home to save my mom and here I am, moping around, feeling sorry for myself instead of contributing to helping the people who are trying to bring her home. Gaby is pulling a pan

of bars out of the oven.

"Gaby, how can I help?" I ask.

"Kate, really you don't have to help. We have enough staff to manage," she says.

"Gaby, these people are all here to help Chase and my father get my mom back. I need to do something to contribute. What can I do?"

"Well, I can use an extra pair of hands," she says kindly. "Can you slice onions, peppers, and mushrooms? We're baking pizzas, lots of pizzas for this evening, and I could really use the help."

The afternoon flies by. Gaby has made dough, from scratch, and we spend the early evening topping and baking the fresh pizzas for the crews. Gaby and I are slicing the last of the pies when Chase walks in. I feel his eyes on me and turn around.

"Gaby, excuse us," he says before capturing my lips with his own.

"Baby, we've had the first good news today. We have eyes on all of the prince's homes and businesses and are tracking anyone that contacts him. He's been in constant communication with a phone on the Gulf. We're getting close to finding her, Baby," he says, pushing the hair from my face. He looks tired, and I pull him close hugging him.

Carlos peeks his head into the kitchen. "Chase they've got verbal confirmation of her location," he says. Chase guides me into the living room and tells Carlos he needs to talk to the guys about getting a visual confirmation, leaving us alone for a short while. My dad looks as though sleep has eluded him for days. I sit on the couch, and he takes a seat next to me. "I wish to hell we would have had Chase's technology the first time she disappeared," he says to me.

Chase comes back into the room and announces that the men have solid verbal confirmation on her location. "She's being held in a home in Miami. They have an address and are in the process of getting eyes on the exact location to get visual confirmation. It won't be long, now. Carlos, we're going to need to discuss a few details about the extraction.

I realize whatever they are going to talk about is nothing that he wants me to hear and head upstairs. I try to read, but am unable to focus. Finally giving up and putting the novel aside, I succumb to exhaustion.

I wake to Chase rubbing my shoulders and kissing my hair. The length of his body feels comforting next to mine.

"Baby, wake up," he says.

"I must have fallen asleep. What time is it?" I ask.

"It's late... just after two a.m. We've got your mom, Baby. She's on her way home," he says. I turn towards him and realize he's still fully dressed and probably has not been to sleep, yet.

"Oh, my God, Chase. Thank you," I say unable to stop the flood of tears from falling down my face.

"Baby, it's okay. She's fine. Our teams took her to the airport, and she should be landing in about an hour," Chase says.

"Is my dad still here?" I ask.

"He shakes his head. No, he's been up all night helping with the ops in Florida, but he wanted to be at the airport when she lands, so I sent him and Jay's team by helicopter to bring her back," he says.

"Do you want to get some sleep? I ask, realizing how tired he looks.

"No, Baby. I want to make sure your mom is okay and doesn't need a physician once she arrives. Once I know everything is fine, I'll get some sleep. Things happened tonight in the process of getting your mom out, Katarina. Do you want me to share these with you or do you wish to see the papers and wonder what happened?" he asks, his eyes searching mine.

"I want you to tell me, Chase," I say, willing myself to stay calm.

"The house your mother was being held in was a drug haven, and Carlos and I had it overtaken by our teams. There were multiple men in and around the house guarding your mom, and you will at some point read that they were killed in an explosion caused by gasses produced by the meth they were cooking in the home," he says.

I take his face in my hands and kiss his lips gently. "I love you so very much Chase, and I can't tell you how much I appreciate you getting my mom back and for protecting our family," I say, trying my best to conceal the questions that rise in my subconscious.

The relief in his eyes is evident, and his jaw seems to relax as he pulls me close, holding me tight to him. "I love you so much, Katarina. I didn't want to subject you to this, but you told me you wanted me to be honest with you. I wasn't sure how you would react to what we had to do, Baby."

"You're in no danger of losing me, Chase. I love you, and I was the one that told you I would not think any less of you or my dad for doing what you needed to get my mom home," I say.

"I've extended an invitation for Carlos to stay here tonight so he and your mom can catch up. If all goes as planned, we will still be leaving for Aruba tomorrow," he says, running his finger across my lips before kissing me. "Baby, let's go downstairs, they should be here any minute."

My dad leads my mom into the foyer. She appears disheveled and her eyes are puffy from crying. I race to embrace her and hold her tight, unable to control the tears of relief that stream down my face at the sight of her. I look up and see the tenderness in my dad's eyes when he looks at my mom. He appears weary, and I hold out my arms and embrace him in a hug. "Thank you for getting my mom back," I say, unable to keep the tears in check. He leans down and wipes them from my eyes.

"You're welcome, Katarina. There is nothing I wouldn't do to keep my family safe," he says. I see that Chase is giving my mom a hug and Gaby is not to be left out, capturing my mom in a giant hug, as well.

It is odd seeing my parents together. My dad's arm is wrapped possessively around my mother's shoulder the entire time we talk. My mom tells us how she was getting ready to be picked up and answered the doorbell. She was immediately overpowered by two men. They put a cloth of some sort over her face and when she came to she was locked in the basement of a house. She said no one told her why she had been kidnapped and that once she heard Chase's voice on the phone, her hope was restored. I capture his eyes with mine in silent appreciation recalling my repulsion at the conversation with her captors. They did not hurt her, but she overheard one of them say they had to wait for an order before taking her out. She was asleep when she heard gun shots fired upstairs, and then lots of shots. I glance at Chase and my dad, but they are not giving anything away. *Did they blow up the house to cover up the shootings? Why didn't he tell me that?* Chase excuses himself to take a call and when he returns he looks relaxed. Everything is completed for the night. "Prince Alfreita has the message," he says to my dad. "Karissa, I'm so very sorry that you went through what you did. Prince Alfreita is seeking retribution for his monetary losses of last year. He still believes that I had something to do with what happened on his ship. Carlos and I are working on a plan to mitigate this in the future, but until we do I have assigned security around the clock again." She groans, but does not argue. "Karissa, it is for your safety and this time security will not be dismissed until Carlos and I know you are not at risk. We never would have allowed you to be without security except the Middle East situation had stabilized. Katarina and I are leaving for Aruba in the morning. You are welcome to stay here as long as you like. I think we're going to retire for a few hours of rest before our flight leaves," he says.

My parents are not up when we wake, so I leave them a note to give us a call a little later in the day. The flight over is uneventful, and I read a novel while Chase sleeps almost the entire duration having gotten a minimal amount of sleep in the past few nights. When we arrive on the island, we are driven to the resort. Chase guides us to the towers and to the same penthouse suite where we stayed two months ago. As we enter, I am enthralled with the arrangement on the table. There must be at least three dozen white calla lilies surrounded by an array of greenery in a beautiful burgundy crystal vase. I turn, and he is looking at me with that intensity I've seen before.

"Chase, they are amazingly beautiful. I don't think I will ever see a calla lily and not think of you," I say.

We spend the afternoon strolling along the beach. We pass a vendor selling body boards, and Chase buys two from the elder gentleman. "I've never been on one of these," I say. "Let's drop our stuff off by the lounge chair," he says. I slide out of my sandals and unzip the transparent cover up and turn around to put it on the seat so it does not wrinkle. I feel the intensity of his stare. "Did you wear that suit to intentionally provoke me?" he asks.

"Does that mean that you like it?" I ask, feeling myself moisten, and my skin begins to heat.

"I most certainly do, it looks great on your ass, but I'm not sure if I enjoy sharing the view," he says.

I smile. "My butt is quite partial to you and the things you've been doing to it, it's all yours," I say.

"Come on; let's get you into the water," he says, taking me by the hand. The sea is cold at first, but it doesn't take us long to acclimate. "I want you to put the leash of the board around your arm, so you don't get separated from it, and then lie face down," he says holding the board steady and assisting me with it. I feel his hands run down the length of my thigh. "Keep your chin up and let the rest of your body relax on the board. I'll bring you out to where the waves are starting to come in, then as soon as you see the whitecaps I want you to kick your legs and paddle... the wave will catch you allowing you to ride it all the way to shore. "Here, now watch... do you see the whitecaps on the waves?" he asks.

I take my position on the board, tense and poised for the tide.

"I am going to let you go now. Okay, go...," he shouts. I paddle and kick, and pretty soon the wave catches me and I find myself gliding across the sea heading full throttle to shore. When I reach it and land he's right behind me riding a wave of his own with a large smile on his face.

"I loved it. Let's go again!" We ride the waves until I'm exhausted and come out of the ocean feeling exhilarated, but tired.

We pass by two young boys playing in the surf, and Chase asks them if they know how to body board. The young boys do not, so he asks them if they want to learn. "I'll be up in a minute," he says to me and nods at Jay, who is never far away. I know it means that he is to keep his eyes on me. I walk along the beach drying off in the heat of the island sun. On my way back to our suite I can see him and watch him for a little while instructing the young boys, pointing out the waves. They are soon kicking and paddling, catching great waves of their own all the way back to shore... they are laughing and having a great time. I lose sight of them as I enter the resort and head to our suite. The air conditioning is cold to my damp skin, and I peel my wet suit off and jump into the warmth of the shower, relaxing under the multi-showerheads that rain down on my body. I pull the white cashmere robe around me as I dry off and smile as I recall the first time Chase wrapped me up in it. My phone is beeping. I have missed texts from Jenny and my mom.

I hit my mom's number first wanting to make sure she is okay since she was not up when we left, and I have not talked to her since last night. She answers on the first ring. "Sweetie, have you seen the newspapers?" she asks.

I frown. "No Mom, what's going on?" I ask.

"Katie, the story of the explosion in Miami is all over the news. Apparently the house imploded instead of exploding and the reporters are having a field day with that information.

"I don't understand the significance, Mom."

Sweetie, the articles are saying it takes a lot of coordination and precise orchestration to implode a building, versus just blowing it up. Although not much remains in the way of debris, the police were able to uncover remnants that make them believe the house was being utilized as a meth lab. However, the last article I read is speculating on how the house would have most definitely exploded if meth were being processed in it. The reporters are interviewing experts who say while it's completely possible the house could have contained the materials used in meth production and not exploded, it's highly doubtful. I asked your dad, and all he will tell me is not to worry. I think he is responsible, and I understand that he was trying to get me back, and I will be forever grateful, but..."

"Mom, what is bothering you?" I ask, sounding much more in control and confident than I feel. Chase told me this. He prepared me for the fact that the news would hit after mom had been rescued. But, an implosion would have taken lots of planning after they got the location confirmation. It means the mission was a thoroughly planned and premeditated attack, instead of a rescue that went awry, as I initially thought. Fuck... I feel sick to my stomach, but try to keep a positive front for my mom.

"Katie, my captors had me blindfolded, and when I woke up, I was in a room downstairs. Everything was dark and dank like a basement. They did not take my blindfold off, but I could hear them jeering at me as I came to. They were talking about raping me and other vile things that I don't even want to share with you. They would have done just that and more if Chase had not insisted on my safety and demanded that they put me on the phone. If he had not asked the questions he did and threatened them with mafia exposure, I believe they would have done whatever they wanted with me. They were pissed when they got off the phone. They told me that as soon as the deal was done, they were going to make me suffer for making them wait." I can hear her sobs and realize she is trying to hold them back. I wish I could hold her in my arms.

I feel even sicker and catch my breath trying to be strong for her. "Mom, calm down, please. Chase and Dad were never going to let that happen," I say, trying the best I can to alleviate her concern from halfway around the world.

"Katie, I already know that," she says, and her voice sounds strong and resolved. I am confused. "What I am trying to tell you, is that if Chase had not done what he did, I would have been used in any amount of despicable manners at the hands of these monsters. He ensured with one conversation that I was not assaulted, beaten, raped and degraded until they were able to reach me. But there is more... "

I swallow and mentally try to prepare myself for the worst. "What happened?"

"Katie, you have to know that if I was not rescued I most certainly would have undergone abuse, but after that, I would have either been killed or put into a commercial ship filled with other people who were being shipped as part of a human trafficking arrangement. They thought I was still drugged when I overheard them talking about this, Katie. "

"Mom," I whisper, saying a silent prayer that she is safe. "Like I said, Chase and Dad were never going to let any harm come to you."

"Sweetie, I am not sure you understand everything," she says.

"I'm listening, Mom," I say, although my head is reeling.

"Baby, I just didn't want you to see the papers without knowing what I was going through," she says.

"Mom, I am so sorry that you went through this, but Chase did tell me that there would be stories about the house blowing up and that it was a known drug house and that meth was being produced there," I say.

"Baby, what he neglected to mention is precisely what I know must be at the forefront of your thoughts and fears right now. Make no mistake. He did not tell you, nor did your father tell me, but this was an incredibly orchestrated event, right from the first loud bang that I heard, to the gun shots, my rescue, being placed in the car, and the implosion. I have not talked to Carlos about the reason for the implosion versus the explosion, but my guess is they did not want any neighborhood casualties, but wanted to make sure these men could never hurt our family or me again, and all evidence was lost," she says solemnly.

I realize I am holding my breath. When did my mom get so strong? I try to process this information. It means that from the moment they got location confirmation they were planning the event and it was cold, calculated and intentional murder. It was not in self-defense, but a planned and deliberate murder of those in the house. *They were holding your mother prisoner and were going to brutally rape her and kill her*, my subconscious jeers at me. She is alive because of what Chase and my dad did, and that is what she wants me to understand.

"Katie, are you still there?" she asks, her voice penetrating through the phone, and I realize I have been lost in my own thoughts for a few moments.

"Yes, sorry Mom. I was just thinking about everything that has happened over the last few days," I say.

"Katie, I know it's a lot of information, but I want you to promise me that you will not think any less of your dad or Chase. They did what they had to do to save me. If they had not, I would no longer be alive," she says.

"Thanks, Mom. I appreciate you telling me about what happened. I just need a little time to absorb it," I say, trying to maintain my calm.

We disconnect and I am still engrossed in our conversation when Jenny's ringtone comes through on my phone. I answer it, and Jenny is gently sobbing. "What is it, Jenny?" I ask, fearing that Ty has gotten to her somehow. She does not answer right away. "Jenny, tell me what is wrong," I urge.

"Kate, Ty was found in his apartment this morning. He was..." she stutters and sobs... "He was found tied up and bound to the bed in his apartment. It appeared that someone tried to overdose him, but the paramedics were able to keep him alive and get him to the hospital. Kate, the police found tons of Torzial documents on his kitchen table that were all written on. They demonstrate how he was able to funnel all of the money into the Torzial books."

The hair on the back of my skin prickles and I am suddenly very, very cold.

"He's at the hospital in critical condition, but it sounds as though he will pull through. The only thing, though… the initial reports say he was either brutally raped or that he and his partner really got rough before he passed out. They think he may have been left by an angry partner based on the tearing, but how? Wouldn't I have suspected something if he had an entirely different relationship?" she says. I am trying to absorb this along with everything that has happened in the last couple of days.

"Jenny, it would seem that Ty lived an entirely different life than what you knew about. Who was he laundering money for and why? He could have double-crossed any number of people," I state, wishing in my heart that I didn't believe the bad character was the man I love.

"I guess so," she says.

"Jenny, what do you think happened here?" I ask.

"Kate, I know for certain two things happened tonight. One… I was cleared of any involvement of laundering money through the Torzial accounts, and Ty received the same brutal and painful assault that I did five nights ago. I don't know what the fuck to think. It's like someone knew what he did to me and made everything right. I know it's awful, but there's a part of me that feels like he got what he deserved," she says, and I can tell she is crying softly.

I continue consoling her before we hang up, making her promise to call me back the following day. I lay down on the bed after we hang up, trying to absorb the last couple of days and tears run unconstrained down my face as I drift into a fitful rest. In my dreams Chase and my father are giving orders and all around me people are falling off billowy clouds into a dark, hellish fiery pit. I try to warn everyone, but it is too late. Chase and my father are unmerciful, and anyone that has crossed our family is sent into the burning embers below. My mother and I are suspended over the earth in puffy layers of white clouds, and there is a kingdom laid out in front of us. I awake with a start and try to shake off my dream. Chase is working on the balcony, and he looks relaxed for the first time in a couple of weeks. I recall his insistence on getting my mom to come to our house, moving his dad's loved ones, rescuing my mom and making sure Jenny is no longer at the mercy of Ty now or in the future. My heart expands with the love I feel for this man.

I am dressed for the evening in a sundress and sandals and just finishing my hair when Chase gets out of the shower. He is entirely comfortable in the nude. I find myself mesmerized as I watch him use the towel to dry the lean muscular physique of his torso, abdomen, and powerful thighs. He is rippled with muscles, and when he stands, he is erect. His eyes connect and capture mine. Hot, molten, and filled with desire... I moisten, and my skin becomes heated as I watch him move.

"Baby, I want to take you out for the evening, bring you back up to our room and make love to you the way we did the first time," he says, pulling me into his body and kissing the side of my neck. He leaves me wanting but filled with anticipation of the evening to come which only inflames my desire for him.

We walk from our tower to the main entertainment area of the resort. The night is warm, but the breeze keeps us cool. Chase leads us to the bar where we first met and gives the bartender a collegial handshake before he orders a glass of wine for each of us.

"Do you know everyone here?" I ask as we move away from the bar with our drinks.

"I try to, Katarina. They work hard for our companies, and I enjoy getting to know them," he says, leading me through the lounge to the table we had dinner at the first night we met.

The lights which held me captive the first time are twinkling over the ocean. A live band is setting up and begins to play while we enjoy our wine. A short while later the waiter brings our meal. Bay scallops and black truffle. I smile, remembering it was our first meal together. As we finish eating, Chase stands to take my hand. "Dance with me, Katarina," he says, and I let him guide me onto the dance floor. He holds me close, and I can feel the beat of the heart I love against my cheek. I breathe in the fresh, clean scent of soap from his shower as I'm guided to the slow and sultry beat.

"Baby, do you remember the first night we met, our first dance? The way you felt in my arms was like heaven. On the way back to the states you wanted to know what you were to me. All I could think of was that I wanted you to be mine. I still want you to be mine, but always...through good times and challenging times. I want you to be the woman I wake up with every morning and make love to at night, Katarina. I want you to be mine in every sense of the word. I love you with all of my heart, and I want you to be my wife." He is holding me close, and I can hear the pounding of his heartbeat. The heart I love.

"Will you marry me, Baby?" he asks, his deep green eyes searching my own as he slips a band of white gold that holds a magnificent princess cut diamond in its center onto the ring finger of my left hand. The band begins to play the song we first danced to, and I realize that even in this, everything has been orchestrated right down to the finest of detail.

DOWNLOAD a free copy of my exclusive story, "A Promise" to receive updates, sneak peeks and fun and games through my newsletter.

WHEN KATARINA LEARNS the stark truth about the violent realities of Chase and her father's world will she still take the plunge and say I do? Read Degrees of Control to find out what happens next!

THANK YOU

Thank you for reading Degrees of Acceptance. Reviews help other readers connect to books they may love. Would you be willing to help your fellow readers learn what you loved about Chase and Katarina? If so, please leave a review.

ACKNOWLEDGMENTS

Wayne, my husband, thank you for always believing in me, supporting my passions, and helping me make my dream come true.

My parents and family have been a steady reminder that you can achieve your goals with determination, hard work, and commitment. Thank you!

Karla, my dear friend, who read the first book first and encouraged me to keep going, and who recommended getting other beta readers, because "You can only read a book for the first time once." Thank you for your unconditional support through all the insanity!

A special thank you to all the people who diligently bring all the aspects of these novels together. It takes an army, and I may be a bit biased, but this team is fantastic!

Debbie, my amazing street team, and all the groups, bloggers, and book lovers who spread the word about these stories, thank you!

Via's House of Vixens, is a "private" Facebook group for readers and fans to connect. If you would like to be part of this group, request to join for loads of fun!

I hope you continue reading Degrees of Control to find out what happens next with Chase and Katarina!

ABOUT VIA MARI

Contemporary romantic suspense author Via Mari likes to keep her readers on the edge, fanning themselves as the action unfolds and the heat rises. Her books, featuring the most handsome, intense males, exemplify extreme romance, with powerful men who will stop at nothing to protect the women they love.

Via was raised in both the United States and United Kingdom. Since childhood, she has enjoyed reading books that carry you away. In fact, you can still find her in the early hours of the morning, curled up in an overstuffed chair by a crackling wood fire, reading a page-turning novel, especially during the harsh winters of the Midwestern United States.

When not writing, Via spends her days with her husband. She enjoys gardening, shopping at the local farmers market, and walking in town or around a big city. And she loves traveling to research her next novel.

She also loves interacting with her readers, so feel free to connect with her on the following social media sites! If you want to stay updated on the latest releases and claim a copy of an exclusive story, **sign up for her newsletter.**